Juneau Black

Mirror Lake

Juneau Black is the pen name of authors Jocelyn
Cole and Sharon Nagel. They share a love of excellent bookshops, fine cheeses, and a good murder (in
fictional form only). Though they are two separate
people, if you ask either one a question about her
childhood, you are likely to get the same answer.
This is a little unnerving for any number of reasons.

Mirror Lake

Mirror Lake

A SHADY HOLLOW MYSTERY

Juneau Black

VINTAGE CRIME / BLACK LIZARD

Vintage Books

A Division of Penguin Random House LLC

New York

FIRST VINTAGE CRIME/BLACK LIZARD EDITION,
APRIL 2022

Library of Congress Cataloging-in-Publication Data
Name: Black, Juneau, author.
Title: Mirror lake / Juneau Black.
Description: First edition. | New York : Vintage Crime/Black Lizard, 2022. |
Series: The Shady Hollow mystery series ; 3.
Identifiers: LCCN 2021035892 (print)
Subjects: GSAFD: Novels.
Classification: LCC PS3602.L293 M57 2022 (print) | DDC 813/.6—dc23
LC record available at https://lccn.loc.gov/2021035892

Vintage Crime/Black Lizard Trade Paperback ISBN: 978-0-593-46630-8
eBook ISBN: 978-0-593-46631-5

Book design by Nicholas Alguire

blacklizardcrime.com

Printed in the United States of America
10 9 8 7 6 5 4 3 2 1

Author's Note

Welcome, dear reader! You have happened upon the charming village of Shady Hollow, a place where rabbits and raptors, squirrels and snakes live together in civilized accord . . . with only the occasional murder to mar the peace of daily life.

Some of you have visited here before, and you therefore know that it is pointless to question too deeply the mechanics of this town. If a moose pours a mug of coffee for a sparrow sitting at the cozy counter of the local diner, why not focus on the friendliness of the gesture, rather than the logistics of dish size or seat height? In fact, it is best to think of the characters within as ordinary folks, just like you and me. For, no matter what appearance they have, they are indeed *very* like us on the inside.

So, with that note, enter in, new and old friends. It's time to return to Shady Hollow.

Cast of Characters

Vera Vixen: *A cunning, foxy reporter with a nose for trouble and a desire to find out the truth, no matter where the path leads.*

Lenore Lee: *This dark-as-night raven runs the town's bookshop, Nevermore Books, and has a penchant for mysteries.*

Chief Theodore Meade: *Bears make excellent law enforcers: big, brawny, and belligerent. But Chief Meade seems singularly uninterested in solving crime when he could be fishing.*

Deputy Orville Braun: *This large brown bear is the harder-working half of the Shady Hollow constabulary. He works by the book. But his book has half the pages ripped out.*

Dorothy Springfield: *A sweet but somewhat eccentric rat. She's been known to believe in all manner of unbelievable things.*

Edward Springfield: *Dorothy's kindhearted and supposedly deceased spouse who nevertheless appears to be quite alive.*

Walter Fallow: *Mirror Lake's esteemed lawyer, who has connections to the Springfields . . . and just about everyone else.*

BW Stone: *This cigar-chomping skunk of an editor of the Shady Hollow Herald. BW ("Everything in black and white!") loves a good headline.*

Joe Elkin: *This genial giant of a moose runs the town coffee shop, the local gathering spot. If gossip is spoken, Joe has heard it.*

Bradley Marvel: *A famous author of thrillers who sticks around town long after his business has ended.*

Arabella Boatwright: *This rat runs Mirror Lake's library, and she knows every secret on the shelves.*

Gladys Honeysuckle: *As the town gossip and busybody, there's nothing Gladys doesn't know. She hates to be scooped on a juicy tidbit.*

Sun Li: *This panda is a former surgeon and current chef. He runs the Bamboo Patch, serving vegetarian dishes to die for.*

Howard Chitters: *Once a humble accountant and now the de facto head of the local sawmill, Chitters is an object lesson in how murder can shake up a routine.*

Barry Greenfield: *A senior reporter at the Herald. This old hare has seen it all, and he remembers it all, too.*

Geoffrey and Ben Eastwood: *These hospitable chipmunks operate the local bed-and-breakfast, which can also serve as a hideout.*

Lefty: *This masked raccoon lives in the shadiest part of Shady Hollow. Whatever the game is, Lefty always knows the score.*

Ambrosius Heidegger: *Professor of philosophy and general know-it-all, the owl is the smartest creature in the forest and never lets anyone forget it.*

Philomena Ambler: *The law in the nearby town of Highbank. This bobcat is on a first-name basis with a notorious local criminal, and she knows where the bodies always turn up.*

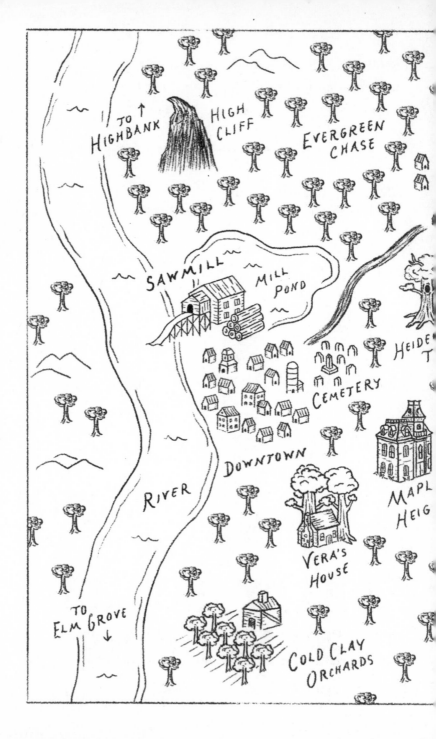

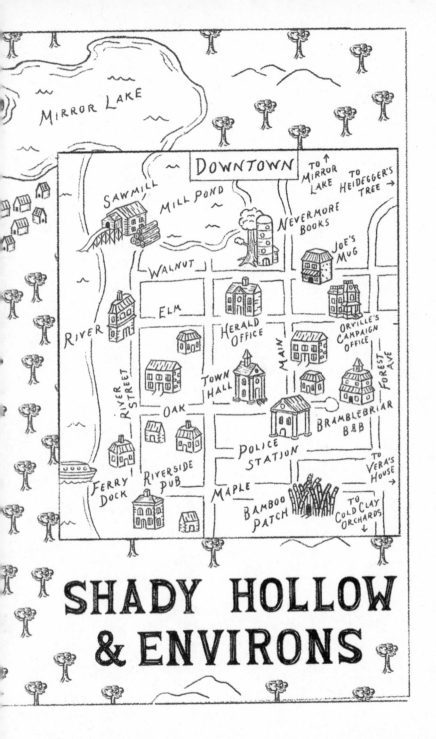

MIRROR LAKE

DOWNTOWN
TO MIRROR LAKE
TO HEIDEGGER'S TREE →

SAWMILL
MILL POND
NEVERMORE BOOKS
JOE'S MUG

WALNUT

ELM

RIVER

RIVER STREET

HERALD OFFICE

ORVILLE'S CAMPAIGN OFFICE

FOREST AVE

MAIN

OAK

TOWN HALL

BRAMBLEBRIAR B&B

FERRY DOCK

RIVERSIDE PUB

POLICE STATION

TO VERA'S HOUSE →

MAPLE

BAMBOO PATCH

TO COLD CLAY ORCHARDS

SHADY HOLLOW
& ENVIRONS

Mirror Lake

Chapter 1

I t was mid-October in Shady Hollow, a glorious time of year that showed the small village to its best advantage. The many trees were gold, red, and yellow, blazing colors wherever a creature looked. It was also the time of the Harvest Festival, an annual event that most residents of Shady Hollow looked forward to all year. It took place at the town park by the river, and there were activities for everyone. There were apple bobbing for the little ones (the apples, of course, were provided by Cold Clay Orchards) and a wide variety of booths with tasty foods of all kinds. Sun Li, the panda who owned the best restaurant in town, the Bamboo Patch, was proudly serving his renowned pumpkin soup. There were also tables laden with local cheeses, ciders, and pies.

Vera Vixen, local reporter by choice and local sleuth by accident, was one of the many Shady Hollow residents who looked forward to the festival. She and Orville Braun, the hardworking deputy of the town's two-bear-strong police force, had planned to spend the day together at the event.

As Vera and Orville wandered among the display tables, they greeted their friends and neighbors. They nearly ran into Gladys Honeysuckle, Vera's colleague at the Shady Hollow *Herald*. Gladys was darting in and out of the crowd, her wings beating so fast they became a blur in the air. All the while, Gladys chatted with folks and gleaned far more gossip and information than anyone else would have dreamed.

"Oh, Vera!" the hummingbird called. "There you are, and with Deputy Braun as well. My, my, my. You two are getting cozy, aren't you?"

Suppressing a sigh, Vera said, "It's not news that Orville and I have gone on a few dates."

"No," Gladys agreed with some deflation in her tone. "It's not news. Unless you want to make some sort of . . . announcement?"

"Nothing comes to mind," Orville replied. His expression was mild, even a little stupid. When she'd first met Orville, Vera had thought he wasn't the brightest. She'd quickly come to learn that, while he had a very different approach to the world, Orville was much, much smarter than he looked. It was one of his best tools as an officer of the law. (His other tools were sheer size, four massive paws, and a jaw that could snap a pine sapling in half.)

Vera and Orville moved through the festival grounds and stopped at a table where two chipmunks were sitting. Geoffrey and Benjamin Eastwood ran the town's bed-and-breakfast, which was located on a lovely cul-de-sac just off Main Street. Ben was offering cookies to passersby, and Vera smiled when he called her name.

"Miss Vixen, you're a connoisseur of treats," he said. "Try my maple cookies. I only bake them in fall and winter."

He gave one each to Vera and Orville. Crunchy granules of maple sugar studded the cookie's top, like a particularly delicious autumn frost. Vera nibbled the leaf-shaped treat with relish.

"*Real* good," Orville said, licking the last of the sugar off his paw.

"Then have a second," Geoffrey insisted, reaching past his husband to offer another cookie. "We've got seven dozen, after all!"

"That won't be enough," Vera predicted. The cookies would pair excellently with a cup of strong coffee, maybe one with a stick of cinnamon in it and a dollop of whipped cream . . .

Dreamily, Vera told the Eastwoods goodbye and walked off with Orville, delighted by the fine day, the blue sky, and the general bounty surrounding them.

Moments later, they waved to Howard Chitters, the director of the sawmill, Shady Hollow's largest business. He was accompanied by what looked to be an invading horde of mice but was in fact just his immediate family.

Vera chatted with Mrs. Chitters and her young daughter Moira for a few minutes, exchanging pleasantries and guessing who would win the bread-baking competition this year. When Vera said goodbye to her friend, she turned her attention back to Orville. "Shall we go find the Nevermore table?" she asked. Shopping for books was perhaps the greatest treasure hunt there was.

But Orville didn't reply, because his attention was elsewhere—he was staring at the cider tent, which was a very popular destination on this crisp, sunny day. Vera followed his gaze and spotted Theodore Meade, the Shady Hollow chief of police. More significantly, Meade was Orville's boss. Meade clutched a mug of cider in one huge paw and was clapping Howard Chitters on the back with the other. This friendly gesture nearly sent the small mouse into the air.

Orville's usually pleasant expression was missing; in its place was a mask of anger that Vera had seen only once or twice. Before she could ask him what the problem was, the police bear began muttering, "What is he doing here? He *promised* to take a solo shift at the station today. I never ask him for anything, and the one time I do . . ." Orville trailed off, sputtering.

Before Vera could gather her thoughts and take in the situation, Orville was striding over to the park's gazebo. A podium was set up for the mayor's speech later in the afternoon. Orville took the stairs in one leap and stood behind the podium.

"Ladies and gentlemice, if I could have your attention, please." Orville's voice boomed out over the crowd. "I have an important announcement to make."

The crowd murmured and whispered. Vera caught a few words here and there. Then she heard Gladys's distinctive loud tone. "*Yes.* I knew it! He's going to propose to Vera!"

A sheep standing next to Gladys tried to shush her when they saw Vera staring. Could it be true? Vera wasn't sure how she felt about it. She liked Orville very much, but they had not been dating all that long!

Vera's musings were cut short when Orville began to speak again.

"As you know, there is an election coming up in a few short

weeks. And while this may be a surprise to hear, I would like to announce my candidacy for police chief of Shady Hollow. I have served this community long and well, and it's time for a change in the establishment. Please cast your vote for me, Orville Braun, for your police chief. Thank you for your attention."

Orville gave a tip of his hat to the crowd and promptly left the stage. Creatures began to chatter excitedly and wished Orville well as he walked through the crowd to Vera. Vera closed her mouth when she realized that it was hanging open slightly. She was completely flabbergasted by this turn of events. She knew that Orville was unhappy with his boss, but she never thought that he would actually do anything about it. Least of all this!

Orville made his way back to where Vera was standing. By the time he reached her, she had regained her composure.

"Vera," he began, "I'm sorry that I didn't give you a heads-up." Orville paused and looked at the fox, trying to gauge her reaction. "It is something that I have been thinking about off and on. I planned to discuss it with you first, but then I saw Meade here at the festival when he promised me he would be at the station, and I just got so mad."

Vera laughed at this, so Orville knew that everything between them was all right.

She said, "Your first mistake was actually believing that Meade would do what he said he would do. Have you ever known him to show up for work on a beautiful fall day like this?"

Orville still looked annoyed for a moment, and then he laughed, too. "You're right, of course, Vera," he replied. "I don't know what I was thinking, imagining that I could count on him to do anything that I asked. Seriously, I was going to wait until he retired in a few years before I ran for police chief, but when I saw him drinking cider without a care in the world, I just lost it."

"You're going to win this election," Vera said with conviction. "You are already doing the job anyway. You might as well have the title and the salary."

Just then, she saw the figure of a skunk standing about twenty feet away. He was puffing on a cigar, and his gaze bored directly into Vera.

She murmured, "Oh, dear, BW wants a word." BW Stone ran the newspaper, and though Vera liked him, he only talked business . . . and it was her day off.

"Skip it," Orville suggested.

"No, he'll just hound me until he says whatever's on his mind. I won't be a minute. Meet you in the music tent?"

"Sure. Oh, actually, I just remembered that I said I'd stop by and see Professor Heidegger today. He thinks someone snuck into his house and rearranged all his books."

"What? Just rearranged? Not stole?"

"That's what he said."

"Heidegger lives about forty feet off the ground," she objected. Granted, plenty of creatures could access the owl's lofty home if they really wanted, but it seemed unlikely that they could do so while Heidegger remained unaware of it. "Oh, well, I'll want to hear all the details. Let's say we'll find each other in the music tent in an hour."

With that, she left Orville and moved toward BW. He was a fast-talking, cigar-chomping skunk who loved a good headline. Vera did not always agree with him, though she respected him, and she enjoyed her job at the paper. But she suspected that this conversation was going to annoy her.

"Vera, how's it going on this fine day? Some news about your special friend running for chief, huh?"

"It was an impulse," she said, wondering if BW was simply put out that Orville didn't make his announcement via an interview with the paper. "He's always toyed with the idea of running, but he made his decision right before he went onstage."

"Not a moment too soon, if you want my opinion!" (BW Stone always assumed that everyone wanted his opinion.) "Meade's a good bear all around, but he's been police chief for approximately seventeen centuries, and it's time for a change."

Privately, Vera concurred. Chief Meade was known more for his fishing skills than for his dedication to duty, and when things got sticky—such as when dead bodies showed up—it was Orville whom the town relied on to solve the crimes.

"Now listen up, Vixen. I've got an idea for coverage of the election."

Vera stood there and wished she had about five more of Ben's maple cookies while her boss outlined his idea. She knew better than to try to respond until he was finished. There was no stopping Stone when he was on a roll.

"The way I see it, you've got an inside track," he was saying. "I want to hear all the info on Orville's campaign. Who better than you? This is going to be a hotly contested election. Meade has run unopposed for years. We don't want the *Herald* to miss out on the story. What do you think?"

"Oh, I don't know, BW," Vera said when she realized her boss was waiting for an answer. "I'm a reporter, and I'm supposed to be unbiased. Folks won't trust my take on things anyway. They all know Orville and I have been seeing each other."

"Why don't you take the rest of the day off and think about it, Vera?" Stone urged. This was not as generous as it sounded since Vera already had the day off to attend the Harvest Festival.

She strongly encouraged BW to go sample some of Cold Clay's hard apple cider, secretly hoping the skunk would sample so much that he'd pass out and forget he'd ever asked her to cover Orville's campaign.

With almost an hour before she was to rejoin Orville, Vera finally reached a table filled with books: the festival outpost of the local bookstore. A small head popped up between two tall stacks. "Morning, Miss Vixen!" a mouse squeaked.

"Hi there, Violet. Where's Lenore?"

"She flew back to the shop to pull some more books. We're really selling them today!" Violet turned then and greeted another customer who had just walked up.

Vera decided to run over to the bookshop to see if she could help Lenore. She didn't think the raven had ever taken off a whole day in her life. Lenore tried to keep the store open as much as she could. There were always creatures coming in to browse and buy a few cards or paperbacks. Lenore hired a few locals to help out at the front counter on the busiest days, but she was the sole owner of the store and, for the most part, handled everything herself. Vera worried about her friend working too hard and never having an opportunity to take a vacation, but Lenore was in good health, and right now the bookshop was her life. It was also an important part of the community in Shady Hollow and provided a place for village folks to gather and talk about books. When Lenore was able to schedule author events and book signings, there was great rejoicing in the town.

In general, there was not a great deal for local creatures to do in the evenings, and attending a book signing was far preferable to enduring a concert at the church, which often featured the questionable vocal talents of Edith von Beaverpelt. Vera had made the mistake of attending one such event when she had first moved to Shady Hollow, and she did not think that she would ever fully recover. Madame von Beaverpelt possessed a squeaky soprano voice, and she was rarely in key. However, her belief in her own talent was prodigious, and Parson Conkers did not possess the backbone to turn down her regular offers to perform, especially because the von Beaverpelts had donated most of the funds to repair the church steeple after it was struck by lightning several years ago.

Walking past tables and through tents, Vera was surrounded by the chattering of cheerful creatures dressed in smart jackets and dapper hats or colorful dresses and frocks, all enjoying the sunny, cool day. She felt out of place and distracted by Orville's unplanned announcement. She'd thought her biggest challenge today would be the sack race on the village green.

She had no doubt that Orville would make an excellent chief of police. It was an open secret that he did nearly all the actual work of the department's daily operations while allowing Meade to take credit for the (mostly) smooth running of the town. Shady Hollow was a peaceful community with generally law-abiding and orderly citizens. Orville had never been a bear to disrupt the status quo. He'd been willing to wait until Chief Meade's inevitable retirement to step up and put his name forth as the obvious successor.

Yet now he'd jumped right into the thornbush.

However, it was one thing to announce a candidacy; it was another to actually run a campaign. And with only a few weeks until the election, Orville had very little time to prepare! He'd need a campaign office. He'd need staff and volunteers. He'd need flyers and pamphlets explaining his positions . . .

"Oh, dear, I'm thinking like a manager," Vera muttered. (In fact, in her school days, she had run campus campaigns.) But she was a journalist now, and she couldn't run Orville's campaign, too. It would be highly improper. But she could give a little advice . . . or perhaps not.

It was all quite confusing. And whenever Vera got confused, two things helped: coffee and the counsel of a good friend.

Fortunately, the first item was on her route. She'd grab a cup of coffee from Joe's table before she left the festival.

A few creatures walked past Vera, heading in the opposite direction and bearing baking dishes that all smelled wonderful. They were likely on their way to the tent where the dessert contest would be held.

A rat said, "I can't wait for the judging. My apple kuchen finally has a chance this year!"

"Did you change your recipe?" a marmot walking alongside asked.

"Oh, no, it's the same as ever. But didn't you know? Dotty Springfield isn't here to enter her cream-cheese coffee cake, the one that took first place three years running. She had to go tend old Mrs. Springfield. She's close to the end," the rat added somberly.

"I've heard that before," a third creature noted. "Adora Springfield is at death's door nearly every month, and Dotty always goes to take care of her. The old lady certainly got lucky with her daughter-in-law. Maybe that cream-cheese coffee cake is the secret to a long life!"

"Oh, Miss Vixen," the apple-kuchen maker said, noticing Vera. "How nice to see you. Good job keeping Orville's announcement a secret!"

Vera smiled wanly, letting the others think what they wished. If only she *had* known in advance. The day could have gone much more smoothly.

Vera arrived at the table sponsored by Joe's Mug, where Joe himself was serving up cups of his special cinnamon coffee. A few sticks of cinnamon hung from his antlers in honor of the occasion. The Harvest Festival was the first time he brewed that particular blend each fall, and eager creatures awaited their turn for a sip.

Vera joined the queue, still pondering the conundrum Orville had put her in. Before she could come up with an answer, Joe was asking if she wanted one or two cups—Vera was a known devotee of coffee.

"Oh! I'll take two, but one is for Lenore."

"Two it is," the moose said amiably. "Nice day for it." He did not breathe one word about Orville's surprise announcement, for which Vera was eternally grateful. Joe was the sort of creature who knew when to talk and when to keep his mouth shut—a rare skill.

"Here you go, Vera," he said, pushing the two drinks toward her. "Now don't forget that my special butternut-squash spice pie is going to be available starting this week. Come by when you have a moment."

Accompanied by a cloud of cinnamon fragrance, Vera continued on to the bookstore. Nevermore Books was situated in an old granary and thus was much taller than the surrounding buildings. Inside, a visitor quickly realized that the store was sensibly arranged so that each floor was devoted to a particular genre, with shelves wrapping the outer walls. An inner railing kept wandering bookworms safe, since the central part of the bookstore was all open air, allowing Lenore to fly to any floor and easily snag the book she wanted. The result was a bright and airy atmosphere, and the store was one of the most popular places in town.

Today, however, it was nearly empty, since all the townsfolk were at the festival.

"Lenore?" Vera called. "Are you here? I've got coffee."

The raven flapped down from her office at the very top of the store. "Vera! Thought you'd be outside interviewing folks about the Harvest Festival. I just needed to pull some more books to bring to our table in the park. Violet's running it, but I thought I'd bring some extra supplies."

"Does that mean you missed Orville's little speech?" Vera passed a cup of coffee to her friend and proceeded to share the news.

Lenore cawed softly in surprise. "My goodness, what are you going to do?" she asked.

"That's why I'm here. I was hoping for advice."

"Well, I'm not sure I'm qualified to give any in this situation. It certainly hasn't come up in the books I've been reading." (Lenore read mostly true crime and murder mysteries.)

"BW wants me to cover the election—from the inside, as it were."

"He would," Lenore said with a huff. She ruffled her glossy feathers. "I sometimes wonder if that skunk has ever heard of ethics."

"All he cares about is selling papers, and he *is* good at that."

"Still, you can't compromise your integrity to help BW. That will hurt your career, and no one will trust what you write anymore, even if it's just a review of the Bamboo Patch's fall menu."

"But how do I explain that to BW? And what do I say to Orville? And what *am* I permitted to do? I want to help Orville if I can. You sure you don't have a self-help book for journalists who are dating aspiring politicians?"

"Quite sure. What you need is a legal guide." Lenore took a sip of the coffee and then said, "Oh, I know! Why not pay a visit to Mr. Fallow? He'll know what you're legally obligated to do, and, more than that, he'll tell you just what to say to keep BW off your back." Walter Fallow was one of the most respected lawyers in the area and lived in the Mirror Lake neighborhood.

Vera smiled. "Now that's thinking, Lenore! I'll stop by his office tomorrow morning. I'll have plenty of time to talk things over with Mr. Fallow then."

Looking at her friend, Vera finally noticed suppressed excitement in the raven's eyes. Vera had been so consumed with her own news, she hadn't even thought to ask Lenore what was happening.

"Hold on," Vera said now. "You're about to burst! What's going on?"

It was most likely something about Lenore's store. The raven worked tirelessly, and the business was a bright spot in the village, where creatures gathered to chat and to look over the latest novels and political thrillers. Lenore was usually reserved, especially in public, so Vera felt certain that some-thing major was in the wind.

"I just got a message from Bradley Marvel's publicist," Lenore said excitedly. "They added us to his new tour at the last minute, and he will be appearing here next week!"

Vera let out an unladylike squeal at this news and gave Lenore a hug.

Bradley Marvel was a hugely popular author who wrote thrillers. They weren't exactly to Vera's taste, but many creatures liked them, and this event would be a coup for the small bookstore. Previously the author had canceled an appearance due to some kind of illness. Lenore had been keenly disappointed, since she'd been forced to substitute a local author—Wilbur Montague, who wrote dull tomes about shipwrecks—and it just wasn't the same at all.

Vera was extremely happy for her friend, who worked so hard and asked for so little. If the star writer actually showed up this time, it would be a very lucrative evening for Lenore and Nevermore.

"Let me help you get ready for the event," said Vera. "That's short notice! But at least after the festival, everything will be quiet around town." This was an eminently logical assumption on Vera's part. It was, however, not correct.

Chapter 2

The next morning, Vera woke in her comfy den-like home and relished the early calm. She'd stayed up rather late the night before, talking with Orville about what he needed to do over the next few days and weeks to give his campaign a fighting chance. Vera figured that giving him a few basic pointers was fine. But it reminded her that a visit to Mr. Fallow was first on her list today.

She strolled through the quiet streets of Shady Hollow. After the festival, most creatures were taking a day off to relax and recover, especially those who'd enjoyed more-potent beverages later in the evening. Sun Li's mulled plum wine had been a hit, Cold Clay Orchards' Spiked Cider ran out every year, and Timothy Leveritt's special aged applejack was always a favorite.

The air was decidedly snappish, with a frosty edge. In a few hours the sun would warm things up, but for now Vera was glad she possessed not only her thick natural coat but also her jade-green hat and scarf—which nicely complemented her reddish coloring.

Mirror Lake was a fairly long walk from the center of Shady Hollow, but it was a delightful stroll through a patch of woodland, and Vera enjoyed the sunlight hitting the amber and yellow leaves of the birches and the aspen. They lit up the whole scene with a special glow.

In the distance, the bright blue surface of Mirror Lake shimmered in the morning sun. A community of homes and businesses was clustered on a few streets along the lakeshore. Mirror Lake was not a proper town, yet neither was it a mere ancillary to Shady Hollow. It had its own feeling—quiet, peaceful, and serene. Much of that was due to the lake itself. Larger than the millpond in Shady Hollow, the spring-fed lake was a haven during hot summer days, and in winter, it became an icy playground. At all times, creatures fished or boated in its waters or strolled along the shoreline.

Many rats called Mirror Lake home. Among them was Mr. Fallow. Vera walked up the pathway to the attorney's office, noting the bright blooms of chrysanthemums and the late roses climbing up the fence. It was difficult to believe that winter would be on its way in a matter of weeks.

Suddenly, someone emerged from Mr. Fallow's office, the bright red door swinging shut behind them. Vera recognized the figure of Dotty's husband, Edward Springfield, a rat of exceptionally polite disposition who always doffed his hat in the street and had a greeting for every creature.

Except on this morning, Mr. Springfield ignored Vera's friendly smile, seeming to stare past her blankly. Then he abruptly turned down the street and hurried in the direction of the lake.

Vera frowned. *How odd.* Was it possible that Edward Springfield was irked by Orville's candidacy for police chief and was taking it out on Vera? It couldn't be! She didn't know Edward well, but she couldn't imagine him behaving in such a way.

Putting the incident aside, Vera walked up to the door, which bore a discreet brass sign that read:

FALLOW LAW OFFICE

WALTER FALLOW, ESQ.

She entered, calling out, "Hello, good morning?"

"Come in, come in," a tenor voice responded from an inner room.

Vera followed the voice to find Mr. Fallow sitting behind a large walnut desk and sorting papers into tidy stacks. He was a sleek rat with dark gray fur and just a few specks of silver on his muzzle. His black eyes were sharp, missing nothing. Few individuals can perfectly embody their professional roles, but Mr. Fallow was one of them. He was born to be a lawyer.

"Good morning. What brings you here today, Miss Vixen? Surely I am not being interviewed for the paper?" His eyes twinkled.

"Not by me," Vera assured him. "This is a personal matter.

Are you busy? I saw Mr. Springfield just leaving, but he was in quite a rush. Is he coming back?"

A frown drew down the rat's silvery whiskers. "I doubt it. Evidently I was not able to give him the news he was hoping to hear. Anyway, he'll be distracted today—word has come that his mother, Adora, has finally passed, rest her soul." He deliberately put aside the papers he'd been holding. "But that is another matter. What can I do for you?"

Vera briefly explained her situation, concluding, "Of course I want to help Orville, and of course I want to do my job. But I don't see how I can do both."

"You can't," Mr. Fallow said with the calm confidence of one who knows the law. "It's a conflict of interest, as you have already seen. However, it is a temporary situation. After the election is over, you shouldn't have any difficulty with your usual duties. You've been covering the Shady Hollow police force for a few years now."

"But what do I tell BW?"

Mr. Fallow gave her a thin smile. "You'll tell him that on the advice of counsel, you must refuse to cover Orville's candidacy or to contribute to any articles related to it. Nor will you publicly express any opinions on the election in general."

"I told him that before," Vera said doubtfully.

"Ah, but now you have the important phrase *on the advice of counsel*. That helps a lot. I'll write up a letter, too, for you to shove in Stone's face when he gets overeager."

"And what if he gets so mad that he fires me?"

"He'd be a fool to do that," Mr. Fallow said promptly. "Everyone knows you're one of his best reporters. But just in case, I'll add a paragraph explaining that it would be *actionable* if you were to lose your job as a result of your ethical stance. No one wants to be on the receiving end of *actionable*."

Vera felt calmer just hearing Mr. Fallow's plan. Lenore had been right, as usual.

Mr. Fallow stroked his whiskers as he leaned back in his chair, saying, "Shouldn't take more than a half hour to write it up. It's a fairly standard document. You've got nothing to worry about."

Just then, a terrified scream echoed through the air outside.

Vera's fur stood on end, her tail puffing out in an instinctive reaction to the sound of a creature in peril.

Mr. Fallow went completely still for a moment, his ears pricked up and his expression wary.

"It came from the direction of the lake," he said in a low voice.

A moment later they both were outside and running toward the lakeshore, intent on discovering who had made such a noise.

"That way!" Mr. Fallow said, pointing to a gracious house by the lakeside. "It's the Springfield home!"

Other residents had heard the sound as well, for a small crowd was already converging on the building Mr. Fallow had indicated. Outside, two creatures stood about ten steps away from each other on the lawn, with the pathway to the porch exactly between them.

Mr. Springfield was one of the two creatures, and he looked even more distraught than when Vera had seen him not half an hour earlier. The other was a female rat wearing a fall coat. A little traveling suitcase was toppled over near her hind paws. She was sobbing, but more from panic than sorrow.

"What's the matter?" Mr. Fallow demanded when both he and Vera skidded to a halt on the front lawn. "Edward? What can possibly have happened since I saw you? And, Dorothy, was that you who screamed?"

Dorothy Springfield lifted her head from her paws and stared at Mr. Fallow with a wild look in her eyes. "Oh, you must help me! My husband is dead! He's been murdered!"

Mr. Fallow's mouth dropped open. The whole crowd shifted to look at a confused Edward Springfield, not ten paces away . . . and appearing very much alive.

Vera blinked, trying to match what her eyes were seeing to Dorothy's words. What was going on?

Chapter 3

For several moments, there was uneasy silence as the crowd struggled to make sense of the anguished rat's words. It was almost as if every creature present was thinking the same thing: *How can she claim that her husband has been murdered when he's standing right next to her?* There was some shuffling and mumbling, and then Mr. Fallow made his dignified way to Dotty Springfield, who was wiping her eyes as she tried to catch her breath.

"Why, Dorothy," the attorney began in a gentle tone. He pulled a crisp white pawkerchief from his pocket and offered it to her. "Edward is here in front of us. What do you mean, he's been murdered?"

Dotty Springfield looked away from Mr. Fallow and stared

at the rat in front of her as if she had never seen him before. She stood up a little straighter and pointed a shaking paw at Edward. With the sort of confidence one uses when declaring the sky is blue, she stated, "This rat is *not* my husband! Edward has been murdered! I swear it!"

There was shuffling and mumbling among the crowd again. It would have been funny if Dotty had not looked so stricken.

Now Edward spoke up as he stepped forward and tried to take her paw in his. "Dotty, honey," he crooned in a low voice. "What is the matter with you? Can't you see? It's me, Edward. I'm right here, safe and sound."

Dotty shuddered and stepped even farther away from her spouse. Edward looked embarrassed as he faced Mr. Fallow.

"Dotty is not herself, as you can plainly see," Edward stated, reaching for his wife's paw only to be rebuffed again. "The trip back from my mother's house must have been difficult. I'll just take her inside so that she can lie down."

Dotty drew herself up and looked around wildly at the crowd.

"Oh, no! I'm not going anywhere with that creature. He must have murdered himself, and I won't forget it," she said firmly, no longer crying. "I want to go to the police station or to the hospital."

This produced even more mumbling among the gathered crowd. "Unseemly" was heard, and "What does she think she's saying?" Rats are generally dignified and discreet creatures. They keep their emotions to themselves and do not act out in public. Such histrionic behavior from one of their own was frowned upon. In fact, rats are extremely kind animals; they do not like to see a creature suffering, especially a neighbor.

With some hesitation, Vera said, "Is . . . is there something we can do?"

Mr. Fallow nodded but said, "Wait a moment, Miss Vixen. We need to talk."

We meaning the rats. Vera stepped away from the main group, keeping a sharp eye on Dorothy and Edward, who were twin islands of stillness in the midst of the shifting, confused crowd. After a whispered consultation among several rats—including Mr. Fallow—the medical squirrels were summoned. It was collectively decided that perhaps Dotty was overtired from caring for her mother-in-law and exhausted from grief. A quick checkup at the hospital couldn't hurt.

Dotty had calmed significantly by this point, and she went with the squirrels quietly. With a hurt and puzzled air, Edward went inside the Springfield house. He'd spoken to a few neighbors but only in short distracted phrases. He wore a worried expression . . . which was to be expected, considering he'd just been told that he'd somehow killed himself.

"Thank you for staying," Mr. Fallow told Vera. "I'm afraid this event has quite disrupted our talk. Would you excuse me for a little while? I'll get back to you about your issue as soon as I can."

She recognized that the attorney was actually very upset, and she murmured some words to let him go without worrying about her. Indeed, Vera's nose was twitching with the scent of a *story*.

Before the crowd dispersed entirely, Vera interviewed a few of Dotty's neighbors for an article in the paper. Most of them agreed that Dotty, while universally liked, was also known for being somewhat eccentric. She believed in things like ghosts and horoscopes, which are not typically tolerated among rats, who praise rationality and skepticism.

As for Edward, everyone seemed truly distraught that he had experienced such a scene. Edward was beloved in his community. He was pleasant and friendly to everyone and did not subscribe to most of the wacky ideas that his wife did. (He was also on the board of the homeowners' association—a thankless task.)

Vera scribbled notes and started to wrap things up. Then one rat mentioned, "Adora Springfield was loaded, you know. Edward and Dotty will come into quite a bit of money now that she's gone."

Vera commented that she was unaware of this.

The same rat replied, "Oh, you didn't know? The Springfields made their fortune in silver mining more than a hundred years ago. When Dotty and Edward inherit Adora Springfield's estate, they will be very well off indeed—that is, even more than they are already. That should smooth over Dotty's worst outbursts with the neighbors."

With that, Vera snapped her notebook shut and thanked all the bystanders for their help. It had been a very strange morning already, and she needed to think.

She made her way back to Shady Hollow, then walked along the main street through the center of town. At a temporary loss for what to do next, Vera's paws led her to a stand of green bamboo growing lush and thick at one side of the street. Only a few leaves had turned yellow so far, and the restaurant on the other side of the living wall was hidden, just as the owner had intended.

Vera walked down the gently curving gravel path, thinking that Sun Li's arrival in Shady Hollow was a fortunate occurrence. Not only did he offer some of the most delicious cuisine in the area; his very presence had opened the settled minds of longtime residents to new ideas. Folks grumbled about the "weird trees" he'd planted when he first opened his restaurant a few years ago. But now they flocked to the place and considered Sun Li an integral part of Shady Hollow life.

The black-and-white bear smiled when he saw her. "Well, good day, Vera. Hungry? I've got some marinated mushrooms you'd love."

"Just tea for now," she said, returning the friendly smile. "I'm a little too stirred up to actually eat anything."

"What's the matter?"

"Oh, just a strange thing that happened." She filled him in on Dotty Springfield's bizarre accusation and the general confusion of the neighborhood at the scene.

"She must be wrong," Vera said in conclusion. "I mean, Edward was literally standing right next to her! But then again, she saw him, too . . . and she still maintained that he wasn't her husband and that her husband was murdered. It's baffling. Have you ever heard of something like this? A creature refusing to believe that their spouse is alive?"

"Hmm. Can't say I have. It sounds like she's very frightened," Sun Li said. It was typical of Sun Li (who had been a surgeon before becoming a chef) to consider Dotty's feelings before the other facts of the case.

"That was plain enough," Vera agreed. "She practically fainted! But she needs to see a doctor, not the police. A murder is impossible."

Sun Li took a slow sip of tea, then said, "I've traveled quite a bit in my life, and I've seen a lot of things other folks would describe as impossible."

"What are you saying?" Vera asked curiously.

"Just that if you do plan on investigating this—and it's intriguing enough to be right up your alley—I'd suggest you start with the assumptions that Dorothy is correct and that her account is reliable. Everyone else seems to think she's made a mistake. And if you think that, too, you'll only discover what everyone else will. Try a different approach."

It was good advice, and Vera thanked him.

After the tea break, Vera made her way to the newspaper offices. The day was still crisp and lovely, but all she could think about as she walked was what she'd witnessed earlier. How strange to believe that your own husband had been murdered when he was standing right next to you. It didn't make any sense at all.

Vera made a quick stop at her desk, right in the center of the busy office of the *Herald*. She wrote up a story on her beloved clackity typewriter and read it over once before getting up to submit it. Then she decided that she could use a pick-me-up and headed to Joe's Mug. The local coffee shop was the heart of Shady Hollow. It was a comforting place where every creature could feel at home and enjoy Joe's fine food and drink.

When Vera entered the café, she was happy to see that it wasn't too busy. Esmeralda von Beaverpelt was working behind the counter and speaking to a customer, another beaver who looked like her spitting image.

This was because the beavers were sisters, and they did look incredibly alike. Not too long ago they'd also dressed alike and acted similarly, too. They were the rich heiresses of one of Shady Hollow's most important families. But after a tragedy shook the von Beaverpelts' world, Esme did something unthinkable—she'd started to work for a living.

Esme had shocked her family by taking a job as a waitress at the humble coffee shop, and she'd shocked the town by being extremely good at it.

Meanwhile, her sister, Anastasia, clung to her past life as a spoiled brat and tried to maintain her image as a wealthy creature of leisure. Judging from the slightly worn appearance of her fancy garb, things weren't going so well.

The sisters remained on good terms, though. They giggled in exactly the same way, and they waved to each other as Stasia picked up her lunch order and strolled to the door.

That was where Stasia stopped, since Vera was in the doorway.

"Oh, Miss Vixen," Stasia said in a pinched, haughty tone. "How do you do this lovely day?" She blamed Vera for some of the family's misfortune, though really Vera had only reported the story.

"I do just fine, Stasia," Vera replied easily, not ruffled at all by the creature's attitude. "Hope you're keeping busy."

"Well, I have some shopping to do in Elm Grove," Stasia said, though it was doubtful that she'd go anywhere near Elm Grove today. "Goodbye!"

Vera let her out and then walked to the counter.

"Hey there, Vera," Esme greeted her in a much more genuine tone. Unlike Stasia, Vera and Esme had become friendly over the past few months. "Dining in or taking out?"

"Hmm, just a takeaway order for me."

Joe's big head popped out of the kitchen to ask if she had heard the latest. Vera looked at the moose expectantly since he'd always shown a capacity for being first to hear gossip.

"Folks are saying Dotty Springfield has gone round the bend," he said in a low tone. "I heard she was shrieking about her husband being murdered when he was standing right beside her. She's always been a little nutty, but this really takes the cake. Folks are saying that Edward should have her institutionalized."

Vera was surprised that the story was already circulating so fast, considering it happened only a couple hours ago and she'd been on the scene. But then again, Shady Hollow was a small community. Vera felt a little sorry for Dotty, especially after experiencing firsthand Edward's cold shoulder outside the lawyer's office that morning. Perhaps there was *something* to Dotty's claims. Vera decided not to say anything about her suspicions to Joe and Esme but that she might discuss it with Orville if she could find the time. As Vera was collecting her coffee, Joe mentioned that Orville had already set up a campaign office in the abandoned storefront on Elm Street.

"The old etiquette school?" Vera asked, shuddering. "I hope the rent was cheap!"

"Cheers to that," Joe agreed. No one was sorry to see the school gone, and, as it turned out, Shady Hollow residents were quite polite to one another without needing any fancy classes.

When Joe saw Vera glance at a pumpkin pie displayed temptingly on the counter, he started to slice a piece for her. "Make it two servings, please, Joe," Vera said, an idea coming to her. "Orville waits all year for your pumpkin pie, and I bet he's been busy this morning. He'll want a treat."

Armed with dessert for herself and Orville, Vera said goodbye to Joe and Esme and walked toward the makeshift campaign headquarters that had appeared overnight. As she passed by, she noticed various residents of Shady Hollow going in and coming out of the office. Perhaps they were interested in volunteering for Orville's campaign. It was certainly good to know that there was support for a new chief of police.

Vera decided not to enter the campaign office herself but instead walked on to the police station, still juggling her coffee and the two pieces of pie. When she entered the surprisingly cozy building that served as the Shady Hollow police department, her cheerful greeting died before it left her lips. Orville and Chief Meade were sitting at their desks on opposite sides of the station, and there was a distinct chill in the air. Apparently they were no longer on speaking terms.

Oh, terrific, Vera thought to herself. Now she was going to have to sacrifice her piece of pumpkin pie so these two idiots would talk to each other. She called cheerfully, "Surprise, boys! Special delivery from Joe!"

Chapter 4

Vera offered a piece of pie to each bear, trying to conceal her acute sense of loss. They both thanked her politely enough, but Vera didn't stick around to discover just how frosty the relations had grown within the police force. After a quick glance at Orville, she dashed out of the police station. Talk about the "murder" would have to wait.

So she went to the hospital, which stood at one end of Shady Hollow's downtown, not far from the winding river that provided much of the town's business.

"I'm here to see Dorothy Springfield, please," she announced to an efficient-looking squirrel behind the walnut reception desk.

"Hmm. Well, the doctor's orders are for her to be kept as

calm as possible. You must promise not to excite her or harass her. Sign here, yes, thank you. Room 304."

Vera climbed the stairs and quickly found the correct room, which overlooked the river. Dotty sat in a bed, which was made up in crisp white linens. A few vases of flowers already decorated the room.

"Mrs. Springfield? It's Vera Vixen. Do you feel up to a chat?"

The rat looked over to the door, where Vera was standing. "Come to gather details for the next big story in the paper, eh? Just like that busybody bird who flits around spying on folks for tidbits in her gossip column."

"Nothing like that. And if you don't want to talk, you certainly don't have to."

"Oh, it doesn't matter." The rat sounded quite resigned. "Come in, sit down. Might as well get the circus started. Were you living here when the *Herald* ran that nasty piece on my attempts to prove the existence of the spirit world through séances? No, before your time. Well, if I could endure the articles that came out then, I can endure them now."

"I take it the séances did not go according to plan?"

"The arrangement of the *candles* did not go according to plan," the rat corrected. "All I can say is that the volunteer fire department was to be praised for their quick response. And I still believe that spirits are among us."

"Mrs. Springfield . . . or is it Dotty?"

"Dot will do, please. I hate Dotty. Lots of folks use it, you know, because it amuses them. A little on the nose, if you will."

Vera pulled out her notebook and pen, then adjusted her wire-rimmed glasses on her nose. "Dot, I'm just trying to understand what happened at your home. It created quite a stir, and you deserve to have your side of the story told."

"No one will believe my side! I'm not even sure I can explain it now. It was a feeling, you see. Intuition. I can't point to evidence . . . not exactly," she added with a more nervous look. "Certainly not without going back there, and I won't do that while *he's* there."

"By 'he,' you mean your husband, Edward?"

"No! I mean precisely the opposite. That rat may look and talk and move just like my Edward, but it's *not* him."

Vera wrote down the words and then paused reflectively. "And this is the part you know by intuition?"

"I knew it the instant I saw him in the foyer."

"But how? I mean to say . . . he looks like, well, Edward Springfield. And he talks like Edward. I myself saw him shortly before the incident. He was leaving the law office as I was going in. I mean, he's wearing all the same clothes and knows the same folks, and everyone else seems to agree that he's Edward."

"Well, they're wrong," Dot said matter-of-factly.

"Why don't you go back a bit?" Vera said slowly, keeping her mind as open as possible. "Tell me how that day began."

Dot sighed. "I had to wake up extremely early to catch the upriver ferry from the dock at Cedar Creek Junction. That's the closest stop to where Mrs. Springfield—Edward's mother, you know—was living after her retirement. Adora had a beautiful home on a bluff overlooking the valley, and she loved it there. Even while she was sick, she said the view helped her more than any doctors." Dot cast a sad look around the hospital room, and Vera nodded to show that she was listening.

"Well, she'd passed away the previous afternoon. I made the necessary arrangements, which was easy, as we'd all been expecting the moment. I sent word to various folks who needed to know."

"Who was that?"

"Oh, let's see. I sent a wingmail to Edward to tell him the news and that I'd be home as soon as I could. As the crow flies, it's only a couple hours, so I knew the message would get there in plenty of time. Mr. Fallow—he's in charge of the disposal of the estate. The administrator at the mine headquarters, so they would be aware. Parson Conkers, so he could prepare for the funeral service. That sort of thing. I didn't think I'd actually be able to leave the next day, but I was very eager to get home. I didn't want Edward to be alone with such sad news on his mind."

"So you got the first ferry of the day?"

"Yes, it leaves before dawn. And it was on time landing on the north dock, which is the one I always use, as it's closest to Mirror Lake."

Vera nodded, scribbling down all the details.

"I hurried home along the usual path and came up the steps of the house, and I tell you . . . that's when I felt something was dreadfully wrong. I opened the front door, and that's when I *knew* things weren't right."

"How did you know that?" Vera asked, looking up to catch Dot's haunted expression.

"Well, I'll tell you about the one piece of hard evidence I have. When I stepped into the foyer, I noticed that the rug was wrinkled and off-center. I'd been gone for a couple weeks, and naturally the house was rather unkempt. But Edward knows I'm particular, so it should come as no surprise that I put down my travel case and started to straighten the rug right away.

"I lifted up the corners to do so, and I was horrified to see that it was stained and sticky underneath. I examined the stain, and it smelled like blood! In that moment, I knew my poor husband was dead. And that was the moment I saw *him*." The last word was spoken with such loathing that Vera shivered instinctively.

"You mean . . . a rat who looks exactly like Edward but isn't?" Vera asked, to be absolutely clear.

"Yes. He came out of the parlor room with a big mean smile on his face. 'You've come home, how grand,' he told me. 'I've been waiting for you.' And then he started advancing toward me. Well, I screamed and ran out of that house, and I'd do it again."

"And that's when everyone ran to your lawn and saw you and . . . the other rat standing there." Vera wasn't even sure how to talk about Edward in this way.

"Yes. Thank goodness it was daytime! If it had been night, I'd never have seen the blood, and no one would have come so fast to keep that hideous creature away from me."

"You can't stay away from your home forever," Vera noted.

"I'll stay away as long as he's there," Dot declared. "A hospital room is better than a grave."

Vera sat back, disturbed by Dot's pronouncement. Actually, the whole conversation was upsetting. Could any part of Dot's story be true?

"You think I'm crazy, like the others," the rat said, sounding more sad than upset. "'Oh, here comes dotty Dotty,' they whisper behind my back. But not so quietly that I can't hear!"

"Regardless, announcing that your husband is dead while he appears to be alive is quite an accusation, Dot. You have to understand how it sounds to others, especially without any proof . . ." Vera paused. "But you mentioned blood. What if I go to the house and verify that?"

Dot gasped. "You can't do that! He'll never let you in, and he certainly wouldn't let you poke around and peek under the rug. You'd be putting yourself in incredible danger!"

Vera twitched her long nose, a habit when she was thinking. "It's only dangerous if Edward knows someone's there."

"What do you mean?"

"Never mind, Dot." Vera stood up, suddenly feeling full of vim. "I know just the creature to talk to for a little night work."

As Vera left Dot at the hospital, her brain was already teeming with plans. She sent a quick note to Lefty, a raccoon who lived in the gray area between sketchy and blatantly illegal, to meet her at a riverside park near the *Herald* office in one hour's time.

They were unlikely to be noticed there. Lefty was a small-time criminal who was rarely seen during daylight hours. She knew that he would make an exception if there was a job involved. In the past, Vera had hired the raccoon for small tasks that she didn't want to undertake herself. Nothing really illegal, but kind of questionable.

Vera stopped at the office to write up her notes from the interview with Dot and to retrieve her messages. She noticed that one of the notes was from BW and pointedly listed the times when reporters were meeting to discuss the election coverage.

Fortunately BW was not in. Vera didn't want to speak to him until she had the letter from Mr. Fallow in her paw. She wanted to be able to plan what she wanted to say before BW could bully her into covering the police-chief election for the paper. She nodded at Gladys on her way out to meet Lefty.

Gladys looked like she wanted to chat, but then again, she always looked that way. Vera gave her colleague a wave but did not slow down as she trotted out of the office.

For a raccoon, Lefty was extremely squirrelly and refused to meet Vera anywhere he might be spotted, like Joe's or the Bamboo Patch. Therefore, Vera would have to lurk with the raccoon under a tree in the park instead of over coffee or lunch like a regular creature. *Oh, well,* Vera thought, *Lefty has his uses.*

As she crossed the park and approached their meeting place, she saw that Lefty had arrived first. He gave her what was intended to be a rakish smile. "Looking good, Miss Vixen," he commented. Lefty had a regular girlfriend named Rhonda, but he still considered himself to be a raccoon about town, and he was appreciative of all kinds of ladies.

"Good afternoon, Lefty," Vera replied crisply, though she stifled a smile. A compliment was a compliment after all . . . even if it came from a petty thief. "I've got a job for you if you're free tonight."

"Hmm, I was supposed to meet Rhonda's mother at dinner . . . so any excuse would be grand."

"What will you tell Rhonda?" Vera asked. She'd met Lefty's better half, and Rhonda clearly held the reins.

"Oh, I'll tell her that something remunerative came up. She's got a head for business—she'll understand. I'm completely available for you, Miss Vixen."

Vera quickly described the Springfields' house at Mirror Lake. She went on to tell Lefty that she wanted him to sneak into the house that night after Edward was asleep and confirm if there were bloodstains under the rug in the foyer . . . or not. "And let me know if you see anything else unusual. And this is *not* a license to take anything expensive or pretty that you may see. Strictly an information-gathering job, understand?"

Lefty immediately agreed to do as Vera asked, for his usual fee. The best thing about the raccoon was that he had almost no curiosity and rarely asked any questions about what Vera was hiring him to do.

"Meet me here tomorrow morning at six to let me know how it went," she instructed. "I'll bring your payment."

The two creatures parted ways without any of their neighbors observing their conversation.

After concluding her business with the raccoon, Vera made another quick detour to pick up the letter from the attorney, Mr. Fallow, who had messaged earlier that he'd completed the work from the morning. She trotted to his Mirror Lake office in the westering afternoon light, thinking that she hadn't done this much footwork for a story (or anything) for quite a while. Luckily, the weather was still holding—it was a lovely autumn day with bright sunshine and just a scattering of white puffy clouds.

When she got to the law office, she went right inside. Mr. Fallow motioned Vera into his office, where she took a seat across from him. He looked even more serious than usual.

"Here's your letter, Vera," he said, sliding an envelope across the desk. "If BW gives you any problems about it, you let me know."

"Thanks. What do I owe you?"

"Well, this time perhaps you might offer services in kind."

Vera's eyes widened. "As a reporter?"

"Actually as a disinterested professional who's aware of the existence of ethical conundrums." He looked rather distressed.

"The fact is, I need to talk out a few ideas, and just settling for a hypothetical won't do. And none of the folks around here can help me. They're all too close to it . . ."

"Close to what?" she asked.

Mr. Fallow had been futzing with a fountain pen. Now he put it down in a decisive manner, having gathered his thoughts. "Edward has been to see me about the will again. That's twice today; once before Dot's outburst and then again about two hours ago."

Puzzled, Vera asked, "Isn't it confidential?"

"Oh, not anymore. I filed all the paperwork at lunchtime, and the contents are now available for examination. Civic requirement, you see. The public is entitled to know what's happening."

"Then why is Edward concerned about it?"

"First let me outline the will. The Springfield will states very clearly that the bulk of the inheritance will go to Dorothy and Edward but *only* if both are living and married at the time of distribution. Otherwise, if only Dot or only Edward is alive, they get a nice-sized annuity while the bulk of the estate passes to the next generation, entrusted to myself and to the board of directors at Springfield Silver Mining until such time as a suitable heir appears. As of this moment, that's probably going to be their daughter, Hazel Springfield, who's at university overseas. But she will not inherit anything until she's back home and married herself. The will is idiosyncratic and very particular. I could show you all the subclauses, but this is the gist of it."

Mr. Fallow cleared his throat and went on, "Edward is deeply upset, because Dot apparently told the hospital staff that she will make a formal claim to have Edward declared dead, based on her . . . er, evidence."

"She'll lose a lot of money herself if that's the case, won't she?"

"Indeed, but she's aware of that and doesn't care. Edward, though, wants to make a counterclaim that Dot is mentally unsound and therefore can't submit any evidence on her own, because she would, by definition, not be a capable adult. He wants me to agree to have Dot committed to an institution until her mental health improves."

"That's rather a mess," Vera said. She wasn't sure why the lawyer was confiding in her, but she knew he'd get to the point soon.

"A mess doesn't begin to describe it. The Springfields have been my clients for years, and there's never been a hint of trouble. And now, in the space of a day, they aren't talking to each other and the whole estate is in limbo. Edward really got frustrated when I told him that the settlement was going to take weeks at minimum . . . months, more likely. His reaction, in fact, is why I'm taking my next step."

Vera was itching to get out her notebook; she sensed a juicy tidbit here. "What's the next step?"

"Naturally I do not believe Dorothy's assertion that Edward Springfield was murdered," Mr. Fallow said in precise tones that he probably used in court. "Not least because he is very much alive and so upset that the accusation of murder is stirring up such trouble. But I must consider my responsibility to the Springfield family . . . not just my current clients but also past and future generations. There *must* be clarity here. I want witness statements from everyone involved and depositions from those with the most to tell. Most important, I want to proceed with the knowledge that Edward Springfield is alive and well without harming Dorothy's dignity."

"Ah." There was the issue. Mr. Fallow didn't want to hurt one of his clients for the sake of another. "How can I help?"

"I wonder . . . if you might be able to use some of your investigative abilities to learn exactly what Dorothy believes she saw and why she made her accusation. I am very reluctant to involve a doctor at this point—there's too much risk of bias or hastiness. But you are excellent at asking questions and finding what others miss."

Vera smiled. "Way ahead of you, Counselor. I'm already working on this due to my own curiosity. And I've put a couple things in motion."

Mr. Fallow looked interested. "Really?"

"Tell you what. You're not hiring me to do anything, and I'm not beholden to tell you everything I learn, which could be inconvenient later on. But if I learn something about exactly why Dot thinks Edward is dead and has been replaced by this . . . changeling, I'll let you know before I write my articles for the paper."

"Only tell me information that relates to legal matters," Mr. Fallow said. "Use your best judgment, Vera. I've got faith in you. And I think the Springfield family will ultimately be very grateful for whatever you can discover."

"I'll do my best," Vera said, rising from her chair. She took the envelope and put it into her bag. "Well, now to do battle with my boss!"

She was somewhat nervous about going head-to-head with BW on the ethics issue, but she felt very strongly about her integrity as a journalist. The visit with the attorney had given her the strength to uphold her convictions.

When Vera arrived at the *Herald* headquarters, most of the reporting staff had gone home for the day. But the printers were running, and several hares were minding the process to ensure that each newspaper copy emerged clear and readable for the subscribers.

Vera headed for BW's well-appointed office. The eternally busy skunk waved her in when he saw her in the half-open doorway. She sat down in the visitor's chair, clutching the letter from Mr. Fallow in her paw.

"Hullo there, Vera," her boss said breezily. "Say, where are we on the election coverage? This race for chief of police is really going to heat up. We could use an inside creature for our coverage." He was clearly hoping that she'd either forgotten her earlier misgivings or simply didn't have the energy to fight him.

However, Vera was not a fox who rolled over. She cleared her throat and then spoke up. "It's not something that I feel comfortable with, BW. I think that it's important for the integrity of the paper, as well as for my own personal ethics, that I not be involved with the election coverage." She continued on without even taking a breath. If Vera stopped talking, BW would jump in and argue with her. She wanted to make all her points while she had the floor. "I am working on another article, but I'm not ready to talk about it just yet. Also, I don't think there's a story there with that Springfield rat over at Mirror Lake. Just a minor spat between a married couple. No need to put any reporter on it—other than me, that is."

Finally Vera presented the letter from Fallow. BW took

it, read through it with his face and snout scrunching up in annoyance, and then tossed it onto his desk. Vera leaned casually in her chair as she waited for the skunk's response.

"Huh," he said at last. "Advice of counsel, eh?"

"Indeed," she confirmed.

"Well. I certainly don't want to do anything *actionable*," he said, sounding wounded, as if Vera had gravely insulted his honor. "I still think the election coverage would be fantastic with you covering the story, but I respect your ethics, Vixen. I also trust your reporter instincts. If you're not ready to wow me with this story that you're working on, then get your tail over to the police station first thing tomorrow and check out the blotter for a juicy crime story. You can still talk to Deputy Orville about *that*, can't you?"

This last remark was delivered in an acerbic tone, and Vera almost snapped back. However, she decided to quit while she was ahead. She had gotten what she wanted from Stone, and she did not want to upset the apple cart.

***

The next day dawned pink and rosy, with a light mist clinging to the ground. Vera twined a long wool scarf around her neck before leaving her house, happy that it was once again the season for such snuggly accoutrements.

It was so early that very few creatures were out and about yet. This was good, since she had made an appointment with Lefty at the park to hear the results of his nighttime adventure in Mirror Lake. Vera would rather that the general citizenry not be aware of the fact that she sometimes employed Lefty as a "fact finder."

She was pleased to see the raccoon waiting for her in the

agreed-upon place. He looked somewhat worn out, and Vera guessed that he had been up all night—it was pretty much bedtime for him. Lefty gave her a wave as she crossed the park to where he waited.

"Hey there, Miss Vixen," said Lefty. "I've got a full report for you. First of all, I didn't see no blood under the rug, but it was super clean and smelled like bleach, so I'm guessing the rat did a major cleanup. But for all I know it might be spilled ink or strawberry jam that he cleaned. Who knows? Anyway, I snooped around the first floor for a bit, but Edward almost caught me when he came downstairs for a midnight snack. I saw him in the kitchen making himself a peanut butter sandwich. When it looked like he wasn't going back upstairs to bed, I decided to slip out one of the windows in the living room while he was in the kitchen. I got away clean . . . er, except I might have broken a lamp on my way out."

" '*Might* have'?" Vera prodded.

"Okay, I did break a lamp. Edward shouted, 'Who's there?' and came running into the living room, but by then I had gotten out. I waited until the rat was on the other side of the house, and then I made a run for it to the trees on the neighboring lot and booked it all the way back to Shady Hollow."

"Hmm." Vera didn't like this development. "That means he knows some creature was in his house."

Lefty waved it off. "Sure, but he didn't see me, so he can't pin anything on us. I'm sure of it."

"I trust you, Lefty," she said, which were words that had probably never been spoken in that order before. Vera gave Lefty an envelope with his payment in it. "After all, it won't do any harm to have Edward Springfield think a creature is keeping an eye on him. Thanks so much for your help."

The raccoon checked the contents of the envelope and nodded at Vera, and the two went their separate ways. As Vera made her way to the police department, she wondered if Edward would have reported the break-in to the cops.

"Well," she said to herself as she trotted along the street, "I'm headed to the right place to find out!"

Vera strolled down Main Street, noting that several windows had sprouted signs overnight saying BRAUN FOR CHIEF and BRAUN'S OUR BEAR! The bright yellow signs were certainly distinctive, and she was pleased that so many residents recognized that Orville would be a good choice.

When Vera reached the police station, Orville was the only one there, with the exception of an elderly rabbit snoring loudly in the first cell.

"Drunk and disorderly," Orville whispered to Vera. "It's Josiah Leveritt, and he does this from time to time—whenever he gets a little too enthusiastic about tasting the new cider batches each fall. I thought I'd just let him sleep it off."

"Where's Chief Meade?"

Orville made a face. "Down at the printing office. He hasn't had to actually campaign in years, so now he needs signs like mine. I told him not to use yellow. *And* I told the printer not to let him use yellow."

Sensible, Vera thought. "I wish I could take a sign and put it up in front of my place, but you know I can't."

"It's okay, Vera. But if you're not here to talk about the campaign, what are you here for?"

"Oh, the usual weekly column. How's the blotter look? Any interesting crimes reported? I doubt a drunk rabbit will grab readers."

Orville shook his big shaggy head. "Absolutely nothing else.

I actually got a quiet night just when I needed it. Campaigning is like working two extra jobs!"

"Nothing was reported?" Vera was surprised, to say the least. "Not even a theft or a break-in?"

"Nope. Why?" he asked, suddenly suspicious.

She covered quickly. "Well, I need to write up something for the column! Say, what happened when you went to speak to Ambrosius Heidegger about the mysterious book rearranger?"

Orville rolled his eyes. "Oh, that. It was nothing. Just the old professor going a bit dotty . . . er, you know what I mean . . ." He paused, looking abashed at the poor choice of words.

"Absentminded?" Vera suggested, to save him more embarrassment.

"Yes, exactly. Apparently he'd gone to visit his cousins for a couple weeks, and he returned only the night before the festival. He got home at five in the morning—just before bedtime for an owl—and he insists that someone had been in his house, reading books and moving things around. And that his larder was raided."

"Was there evidence for that? I mean, other than Heidegger's memory of where the books were?"

"Of course not!" Orville replied. "Things were a bit messy, true, but he's not the tidiest creature in the first place. I didn't see anything to suggest an intruder, and if Heidegger reported that his pantry was suddenly bare, well, perhaps he just forgot to do the shopping before he left. It was all a waste of time."

"Hmm. I'm sure he just made a mistake. But it's not like Heidegger to make that much of a fuss, is it?"

"It's not like Dorothy Springfield to say her husband is dead," Orville pointed out. "It's not like me to run for office. And yet, here we all are. There must be something in the water."

"Well, I'll keep an eye out for more odd behavior. But I still need a topic to write about for tomorrow's issue."

He grinned. "You could point out that Shady Hollow is actually quite peaceful, thanks to the work of law enforcement."

"Or maybe I'll steal a pumpkin pie from Joe and write about how it was totally worth it."

"I'll have to lock you up if you do, Miss Vixen. Confessing in the paper would be a big mistake, even if Joe didn't report it."

Vera chuckled, but his words made her wonder why Edward Springfield *hadn't* reported the thief in the night or the broken lamp. It was as odd as Heidegger's insistence on a theft that didn't happen.

She said goodbye to Orville and wandered outside, hoping to get some inspiration for her column. The truth was that Shady Hollow *was* a fairly quiet place most of the time, and the newspaper sometimes lacked headlines more exciting than "Acorn Flour Mishap Covers Maple Street in 'Snow'" or "Annual Quilting Gala Announced." It was a source of frequent pain to BW Stone, who dreamed of heart-stopping headlines every single day.

The total lack of crime-based news left Vera without any obvious story to write for tomorrow's edition. However, back at the office, she found out that the rabbit who usually handled the obituaries was home with a bad cold, so she jumped at the chance to volunteer.

"I'll be happy to write up the obituary," Vera said, grabbing the fat news file on the late Adora Springfield. In fact, Vera was eager to delve into the Springfield family's history.

Vera wanted to get a quote from Dot about Mrs. Springfield, something nice and loving to lead the article. But upon arriving at the hospital, she was informed that Dot had checked out.

"She hasn't gone back home, has she?" Vera asked in surprise. Would Dot have changed her mind so soon? Or was Edward able to persuade her that the danger was all in her head?

"Oh, no, Miss Vixen," the squirrel at the desk said. "She moved to a secret location. For her safety and well-being, we're absolutely forbidden to say where." The squirrel then leaned over and whispered, "She got a room at Bramblebriar."

"Ah, thank you," Vera said, "but maybe don't tell that to everyone who asks."

"You got it, Miss Vixen," the squirrel said cheerfully.

Bramblebriar was Shady Hollow's most charming inn. If anyone was doubtful about that, the fact was clearly stated on a sign nailed to the fence outside.

BRAMBLEBRIAR BED & BREAKFAST

SHADY HOLLOW'S MOST CHARMING INN

Not that there's a lot of competition, Vera thought wryly. Still, as she opened the gate and walked up the path, she had to admit that the atmosphere *was* extremely charming. The whole front yard had been planted as a cottage garden and teemed with flowers and fragrant herbs. A wooden porch overlooked the garden. A few brightly painted rocking chairs stood ready for guests to sit down and take in the peaceful view. Bees buzzed lazily around the chrysanthemums and dahlias, which were still blooming.

Before Vera could knock on the cheerful yellow-painted

door, it was opened by a chipmunk who smiled at her like an old friend. It was Geoffrey Eastwood, one half of the couple who ran the inn.

"Why, it's Vera Vixen," he said. "Come in, come in. I've just put a kettle on!" As he spoke, he hustled her inside with a burst of welcoming energy. Once the door was closed, he said, "I expect you're here to talk to Mrs. Springfield, poor creature. She's up in the Blue Room, and as it happens, I was just about to bring her tea, so follow me to the kitchen and then we'll both go up. She's afraid to leave her room, you know. Ben and I are doing our best to let her adjust."

Vera trailed after him, bemused in the wake of his initial speech. "When did she arrive?"

"Last night, around eleven. She didn't want to be seen, hence the cover of darkness. Do you take milk?"

"What?" Vera was startled by the sudden change in subject, but then realized he was adding a teacup to the tray for her. "Oh! No, thank you. Just as it comes. Is Dot the only guest right now?"

"Yes. That makes it easier. We've got some author arriving soon, but that won't be a problem since he's staying only a couple nights."

"Oh, you must mean Bradley Marvel!"

"That's the one. His publicist insisted that he must get the grandest room. Which is the Blue Room, but we're not going to tell him that! As if we'd kick poor Dot out of her temporary home for the sake of some big-city . . . er . . ." Geoffrey stopped, remembering that Vera had also come from the big city.

"Those city types can be overbearing," she agreed with a

wry smile. "But he's an author, so he'll probably be just as quiet as can be. He won't frighten Dot."

He nodded. "Oddly, it's not strangers who frighten her."

"It's only Edward who scares her," Vera noted sadly. "Did she say anything to you to explain more about what happened?"

The chipmunk said no. "I don't pry. Room and board . . . that's what we do here. Anything else is outside our expertise."

Vera wasn't sure if that was a warning or simply Geoffrey's philosophy of business.

Upstairs, Dot opened the door to the vaunted Blue Room and allowed both Vera and Geoffrey in. The Blue Room was in fact a suite (since it *was* the grandest room in the inn), and true to its name, it boasted pretty pale blue walls and deep blue curtains over the windows. A large oil painting of Twilight Falls, a popular subject for landscape artists in the region, dominated one wall.

The sitting room featured a fireplace with a mirror over the hearth and lots of carved wood all around. Through a partially open door, Vera glimpsed a four-poster bed in the next room.

The chipmunk placed the tea tray on a low table near the fireplace and pulled a chair from the corner so Vera could sit opposite Dot's comfy armchair. Dot looked quite at home, and there was no hint that this was the rat who'd nearly suffered a nervous breakdown a day before.

"Geoff, why don't you pull that vanity chair over here?" Dot asked. "You're staying for a cup, aren't you?"

"The second cup is for Vera. She arrived just as I was getting the tea ready."

"Nonsense. You go a fetch another cup and come right back here before the pot gets cold."

"Yes, ma'am." Geoffrey hurried out.

Dot looked over to Vera. "Now you go get that vanity chair. I feel awful with Ben and Geoff waiting on me all the time, and don't you say it's their job. I know it's their job, but it doesn't change the fact that they're being so kind."

During this speech, Vera found the chair in front of the vanity in the bedroom and hauled it out to join the others. She arranged everything and poured a cup of tea for Dot just as Geoffrey returned.

"Sit down, everyone," Dot instructed. "Miss Vixen, I assume you're here on business, but you'd better have a sip first. And eat one of those little white cookies or they'll be gone before you can blink. Flaked coconut, and so delicious. Ben makes them, you know."

"Ben is in charge of all the food," Geoffrey explained. "I'm better with the housekeeping and repairs and whatnot."

Having popped a cookie into her mouth as ordered, Vera couldn't reply, since she was temporarily transported to some mystical land where all was sweetness and bliss and the air was perfumed with honey and coconut milk. The cookie's only flaw, she decided, was that it was far too small.

"Mmmm," she said at last. "I'm going to need some more of those before I leave. They might be better than the maple cookies! Tell Ben he's a genius."

Geoffrey looked as pleased as if he'd gotten the compliment himself. "I'll tell him as soon as he's back from the grocery."

"Now, Miss Vixen," Dot said after they'd all enjoyed a round of treats. "What brings you here?"

Vera took a sip of tea—which was fragrant with a swirl of lavender—and replied, "Based on your account of what happened when you returned home to Mirror Lake, I did some investigating. You might be interested to learn that there's no bloodstain under the rug in the foyer at your house."

Dot's shoulders slumped. "You don't believe me! I knew it. I swear I saw blood—"

"I'm not done, Dot," Vera said gently. "I'm telling you that there's no blood on the floor *right now*, and in fact, the spot underneath the rug is scrubbed totally clean. Not a stain or even a speck of dust."

Geoffrey was following this exchange closely, and he said, "You're suggesting someone removed the evidence Dot saw!"

Vera nodded. "That's my guess. But I don't know when it was cleaned, only that it must have occurred after Dot's accusation and before midnight last night. That's a long period, and Edward might not have been home the whole time. Theoretically, anyone might have snuck inside to clean up the mess. Unless," she added, looking at Dot, "you cleaned the foyer before you went to care for Mrs. Springfield and used bleach or—"

"No, I never use that nasty stuff. Lemon oil and baking soda are the strongest ingredients I use. And my poor Edward was so busy with the mine business that he wouldn't have time for house cleaning. He normally travels to the mine every week or two, you know."

"So someone must have cleaned it last night. I want to see that stain—or lack of stain—in full daylight," Vera mused.

"When did you see it, Miss Vixen?" Geoffrey asked curiously.

She was wary of revealing Lefty's involvement, so she hedged a bit. "The conditions were not ideal, and further examination will help me understand exactly what's going on. I'll go there and speak to Mr. Springfield myself. And if I happen to flip up the corner of the rug . . . well . . ."

Dot's teacup clattered in its saucer. "You must be careful!" the rat told her. "That creature is dangerous!"

Geoffrey nodded, though his voice was much calmer. "All this talk of blood makes me think that something nefarious is going on. Consider taking someone along with you, Miss Vixen. Perhaps your beau?"

"A police presence might not be the best message," Vera said, thinking quickly. "I'd take Lenore, but she's so busy right now, what with the big event coming up. Does Edward have any particular friends in town who might help convince him to talk to me?"

Dot nodded. "Edward was friendly to everyone, of course, but he spent the most time with Stan Mortimer and that group. They had a weekly game night and switched between poker and backgammon."

"I'll look them up," Vera promised, jotting the name down in her notebook.

"You'll probably have to wait," Dot advised. "A lot of Mirror Lake residents are pitching in to help plan the funeral and the wake for Adora. Until that's over, everyone is likely to be distracted. I'm sure Adora would have been pleased to know that her funeral might beat out the Harvest Festival as the biggest event of the season!"

Chapter 5

As she'd promised, Vera climbed the steps to the Spring-field house and stood on the wide porch that fronted the building decorated with gingerbread trim. Potted ferns hung from the beams and large comfortable-looking chairs woven from willow were placed so that a creature could sit and look out at Mirror Lake, which was currently a silvery gray color to match the clouds overhead. She hesitated a moment before knocking, steeling herself for a very frosty interview. She'd come alone, unwilling to wait for or drag along one of the cronies Dot had mentioned.

But when the door opened, a smiling Edward stood there.

"Miss Vixen," he said warmly, "I'm glad you stopped by. I was just thinking about when we crossed paths at Mr. Fallow's office. I was so preoccupied that I didn't even say good morning. I have just been so out of sorts that I must've seemed inexcusably rude. Please forgive me."

"Well, you've had quite a week, Mr. Springfield," Vera said with admirable understatement.

"Oh, call me Edward," he said. "And please come in. What can I help you with?"

"I'm writing an article and the obituary for your mother. Because she was so important to the town, we want to do justice to her accomplishments and really get all the details to put in the paper. If you wouldn't mind, I'd like to ask a few questions."

"Naturally, I'd be delighted. She had a very full life, you know, so there's plenty to talk about. Here, have a seat."

Among the tasteful bric-a-brac in the formal sitting room, light from a nearby lamp allowed Vera to survey Edward. Like so many other items in the house, the lamp featured silver in its design. It had a silver base that was beautifully molded to look like a bunch of lilies bound with ribbon. But its linen shade didn't quite fit; it was oddly small, as if intended for a different lamp altogether.

Vera asked Edward for stories about his mother, explaining that the paper was allotting practically the whole front page to Adora's funeral, her obituary, and a story about her life. Such was her importance in the town's history.

Edward responded enthusiastically and told several stories that Vera never would have picked up from public sources. He wiped his eyes at one point, undone by a tender moment he related about his mother from when he was a child.

"It wasn't just the family she was good to," he added toward the end. "She looked at the whole neighborhood, the whole town, as her family. If she heard about some folks who were scraping for food, she made sure a fresh supply of nuts and dried fruit and extra flour for baking showed up on their doorstep. Didn't make a big scene, never even put a note with her name on it. She didn't want glory. But folks knew it was her."

Vera wrote it all down, feeling the story form in her mind. But all through the interview, the lily lamp kept catching Vera's eye. What was *wrong* with it? Then Vera realized it must be the very lamp that Lefty knocked over during his nighttime excursion.

So she said, "By the way, I wanted to ask if you'd heard about any burglaries around here or even experienced one yourself. This is such a grand house. A thief would be attracted to all the silver you must have here, what with it being the source of the family's business."

Edward only shook his head. "No, no, no. Mirror Lake is so peaceful. In all honesty, I have never worried about this house getting broken into. Is this part of what you're writing for the obituary?" he asked, puzzled.

"Oh, no! It's for another story entirely. I'm always on the lookout for crime to report."

"You'll have to go somewhere other than Mirror Lake then. Rats are too levelheaded for senseless violence."

Vera covered her suspicions with a blank gaze. Surely Edward knew that some creature had busted the lily lamp and escaped through the window. Or did he truly think it was the wind or something like that? In any case, he seemed not to want the idea of crime brought up. Perhaps that was understandable, considering Dotty's accusing him of the worst crime imaginable.

"If that's all," Edward said, still scrupulously polite but

pretty clearly wanting to get Vera moving along, "I have some documents to look over regarding the mine, and I need to talk to the forebeast . . ."

Vera stood up, busily gathering her things. "Of course, I've taken up far too much of your time. Thank you for speaking with me. I've got plenty of good information for the obituary, and once again, I want to extend my condolences on the loss of your mother."

He smiled sadly. "Thank you. I always knew the day would come, but that doesn't make it any easier." In Edward's eyes, Vera caught a hint of deep sorrow, the sort of pain that a typically rational rat would deny feeling.

As she walked briskly out of the parlor, she nearly collided with a badger who was waiting in the foyer, sitting awkwardly in a chair that was much fancier than the creature's outfit.

"Sorry!" Vera yelped, dancing sideways to avoid tripping over the badger's big paws.

He retracted his legs as quickly as he could and tried to stand up at the same time, which resulted in an odd ballet of movements that threatened to go badly, though in the end the badger managed not only to stand but also to doff his hat.

"Excuse me, miss," he said. "I was just waiting for Mr. Springfield and I nodded off."

"You must be the mine's forebeast," she guessed, remembering Edward's earlier words.

"That's right. Clarence Hobbs, at your service." He gave a polite bob of the head.

"Pleasure, Mr. Hobbs. I'm Vera Vixen." He didn't seem to recognize her name, which was a bit of a relief. She went on, "Do you always come here to talk to Mr. Springfield? It must be quite a journey." From all her research, she'd learned that there were several mines, all located in the hills to the northwest—a distance that would take a full day's travel for a land-bound creature.

The badger shook his head. "No, that'd be impractical. Normally I just message the daily reports and Mr. Springfield messages back. Ira—he's a hawk—is employed full-time as a courier. But what with the funeral and all, I guess Mr. Spring-field was too distracted to keep to the schedule."

Before Vera could say anything else, a voice came from behind her. "Ah, Mr. Hobbs, of course! Come in, come in!"

She turned to see Edward standing in the doorway with a broad smile on his face, as though he had no care in the world. The facade was not convincing, and Vera felt another pang of sympathy for the poor creature. Perhaps the reason he didn't report a break-in was simply that he was overwhelmed. After all, only the lamp was damaged and nothing was actually stolen. What if Edward just couldn't face the paperwork?

Hobbs went in and closed the door behind him. Vera stood alone in the foyer, and she looked down at the beautiful crimson rug covering the center of the floor. Without waiting a moment longer, she knelt and flicked back the corner of the rug, then rolled several feet of it into a tube to expose the floor underneath.

The wide oak floorboards were the same as the rest of the room's . . . except for their slightly faded appearance and dull finish, which were unlike the shiny, wax-coated flooring everywhere else. Back in the city, Vera had once needed to clean her own home but left it too late. She'd figured a strong blend of bleach in the wash water would clean everything twice as fast.

Instead she'd discovered that the chemical interaction of the bleach and the wax gave her floor a milky, cloudy coating that never came off.

These floors looked just the same, and Dot had been adamant that she never used bleach. Vera put her nose to the floor and sniffed, recoiling at the sharp odor of bleach. Yes, someone had definitely done a hasty cleaning job here. If there ever had been blood on the floor, it wasn't there any longer.

She rose and started to kick the rug back into place . . . the lovely crimson wool rug with a deep pile.

Crimson, Vera mused. Seized by that thought, she knelt once more and peered closely at the rug. Seeing a slight change in hue near its right corner, she touched the woolen tufts and felt a slight crustiness, as if something was stuck there. And when she pulled her paw away and sniffed, she caught the unmistakable scent of dried blood.

Vera hurried out of the Springfield house, disturbed by the discovery. It lent much more weight to Dot's accusation . . . but even if there was blood, what did it mean? There was still no body, and if Edward was there in the house and Dot was at Bramblebriar, who could have been killed?

Vera thought it would be prudent to visit the Mirror Lake branch of the Shady Hollow Public Library for a few more details about the family. Although she considered it important to support Lenore's bookstore, she was also a regular patron of the library. She used its facilities for much of her research and for some of the many books she read; if she purchased every single book that she read from Nevermore, she wouldn't have money left for anything else.

As she entered the relatively cool and dark atmosphere of the library, Vera felt a familiar aura of calm wash over her. She had been running around for the last two days in a frenzy of activity. It felt good to just breathe and relax in this welcoming sanctuary. Several of Vera's neighbors were taking advantage of the library's story time in the children's department. Other creatures were checking out books at the circulation desk, and she nodded at them. She wanted to speak with the reference librarian, an efficient lady rat named Arabella Boatwright.

Vera approached the reference desk in the main part of the library, where Ms. Boatwright presided. Much as Mr. Fallow looked as if he were born to be an attorney, so, too, did Ms. Boatwright appear exactly as one might expect a librarian to look. She wore a dark dress paired with a bright red cardigan, and her glasses hung on a gold chain around her neck.

The librarian looked up from her work as Vera approached the desk.

"Well, Miss Vixen," the rat greeted her cordially, "what can I help you with today?"

"Hello, Ms. Boatwright," Vera responded. "I have been tasked with writing an obituary for the late Adora Springfield, and I need some background on the family. Would you be able to help me with that?"

"Indeed, I can," said the rat. She took a set of keys from her desk drawer and asked a colleague to watch the reference desk for her. "Please come with me, Miss Vixen," she said, leading the way to a locked cabinet that stood against a wall. "The library has a special collection of local history that is kept locked. It cannot be checked out; however, it is available to look at here."

Vera was thrilled that so much information was available

to her. The Springfields were a prominent family in the Shady Hollow area, so it made sense that their history was documented. Ms. Boatwright selected a thick binder and then directed Vera over to an unoccupied study table.

"Please let me know when you are finished," the librarian said, "and I will return the binder to the cabinet."

Vera spent a good hour leafing through the various materials and jotting down many notes she wanted to include in her article. However, a part of her brain was also on the lookout for clues that would explain something about Dorothy's outburst. She didn't even know what exactly she was looking for, only that there was a missing piece.

Vera thought she'd seen everything available when the reference librarian approached her study table. Ms. Boatwright had another object clutched in her paw, and she looked about as excited as it was possible for a rat to be.

"Oh, Miss Vixen," she whispered, not wanting to disturb the peace of the reading room, "I forgot about this part of the collection. It was in our bindery to be repaired."

The binder was the same dark blue color, indicating it was part of the local history special collection. A label on the front caught Vera's eye: *Founding Families of Mirror Lake*. The fox felt a rush of excitement mixed with wild curiosity. She barely stopped herself from grabbing the binder, but she managed to wait for Ms. Boatwright to set it on the table. Vera thanked the librarian in the same whispered tone.

Vera paged through the new binder, noting the names of the families who founded Mirror Lake. The Springfields were just one of many, including the Rickenbachs, the Mortimers, and the Buxtons. She turned to the section on the Springfields, and there it was: a family photograph taken when Edward Springfield was a child. Vera caught her breath as she gazed at the sepia photograph, which showed a family of four rats. According to the caption underneath, this was a picture of Edgar and Adora Springfield and their *two* sons—Thomas and Edward.

Thomas? Vera was flabbergasted. Who was Thomas Springfield? Vera paused, thinking she must have made a mistake. Everyone spoke of Edward as the sole heir to the Springfield Silver Mining fortune. But if there was another son, shouldn't he be involved as well?

She could not tell which of the rats was the older brother. They both looked bright eyed and happy. So Vera went back to the reference desk with her find and showed the photo to Ms. Boatwright. "Excuse me, but I need to track down another member of the Springfield family. There are only a few mentions of him here."

"Oh, who?" the librarian asked, her eyes lighting up with interest at the idea of another research thread to pull.

"Thomas Springfield. Edward's brother, I believe."

The refined rat lost her composure a little. "Wow!" she burst out, generating a few surprised looks from various corners of the library. "I had no idea there were two Springfield heirs! I wonder what happened to Thomas?"

Vera smiled as she realized that she was in the presence of a kindred spirit. Apparently Ms. Boatwright had a bit of detective in her as well.

"I have no idea," Vera replied, "but I'm going to do my best to find out."

However, an hour later neither researcher was enlightened.

Apart from a few mentions in clippings about the family, Thomas Springfield seemed to have vanished entirely after his childhood.

"Could he have died?" Vera asked at last. "A fever or some illness could explain it."

"Possibly," Ms. Boatwright said. "Our materials come to us by happenstance, you know. It just depends on what gets donated to us for preservation. So the archives are never complete. You could inquire at the church. Or just walk through the cemetery. All the Springfields should be buried in the family crypt."

"That's a good idea," Vera said. The fox returned the resources to the librarian and thanked her for all her help. What a coup it had been to discover that family photograph! She would never have seen it if it hadn't been for Arabella Boatwright. Librarians are amazing creatures.

When Vera exited the library, she blinked in the strong sunlight of an autumn afternoon. The sky was an almost-sapphire blue, with only a few small drifting white clouds. Without consciously meaning to, Vera's paws took her down a few blocks from the library to the shore of the lake itself. The streets ended well short of the water, leaving only an expanse of grass to the shoreline. A small sand beach lay a little distance away. In summer it was filled with creatures: Little ones making sandcastles and burying friends in mounds of sand with only their heads peeking out. Older children leaping into the water and splashing with abandon while parents sat under umbrellas or in the shade of the few spreading oaks. Vera could picture it perfectly.

But this late into fall, only a few residents were enjoying the lake. One rat, dressed in overalls and a wide-brimmed hat, was fishing from a wooden pier, casting a line into the water with steady patience. Out toward the middle of the lake, Vera spotted a couple plying a canoe toward the far shore, using this lovely sunny day for a last excursion before the boats were put into storage for the winter.

It was beautiful but a little melancholy. Vera gave a sigh, feeling unhappy though she couldn't pinpoint why. Perhaps it was just from all the confusion around Dorothy's accusation and the other unsettling changes in town—the election most of all. She hoped Orville wasn't going to regret running to replace his boss. Vera couldn't imagine how BW would react if she announced plans to take over as editor in chief!

Just then, the rat with the fishing pole noticed her staring. Although he didn't know Vera at this distance, he raised a paw and gave a friendly wave to his fellow creature. As he waved, his reflection waved, too, upside down and distorted in the ripples on the lake's surface.

Vera waved back, cheered by this simple gesture. Life in a small town was very different from what she'd been used to in the big city, but she was glad she'd made the choice to move. Little things, like a greeting from a stranger, were surely a sign of a good way of life.

"All this oddness will get sorted out," Vera said to herself, gazing across the lake to the low hills beyond, which were still crowned with the last of autumn color. "It'll just take a little time."

At that moment, Vera remembered that she'd agreed to meet Lenore for coffee that afternoon, partly to help with the last-minute promotion for the Bradley Marvel event (and partly for pure gossip). She'd have to hurry!

Zipping through the small cluster of buildings that made

up Mirror Lake's center, Vera glanced at the distant Springfield house, her eyes drawn to the mystery within. Then the view was eclipsed by trees as she traveled through the small wood that separated Mirror Lake from Shady Hollow proper.

The woods were sunny and bright since so many leaves had fallen. Vera caught sight of a few local teens, one of whom carried a pickax over a shoulder. Vera chuckled to herself. So folks were still going treasure hunting, spurred by rumors following a shocking murder, which Vera herself had investigated. Rumor had it there was a cache of precious stones hidden somewhere in these woods by the murderer, who'd planned to use it to finance their getaway. Of course, no one had found it yet, and Vera half suspected there was nothing to find anyway . . . considering the one who'd supposedly buried the treasure was not exactly the most trustworthy creature in the world.

At a steady trot, she passed through the woods and then by the placid millpond, finally slowing down when she reached the outskirts of Shady Hollow and the first few businesses along the main street.

By the time she got to Joe's Mug, Vera was breathing normally again. She entered and slid into a booth, where Lenore was waiting for her. Vera wordlessly accepted a mug of coffee from Esme, who had mastered the art of placing a hot beverage on the table almost before a body could sit down.

Lenore lifted her own mug in a toast, saying, "I'm a little surprised you made it. I thought you'd pick up a new lead and be off on the trail again."

"I wish," Vera replied. "But this case is barely a case, and I'm not sure where to turn next."

"So you turn to coffee. Well, at least you're dependable."

After chatting for a few moments about the upcoming event, Vera took a stack of printed bookmarks from Lenore, promising to distribute them throughout the *Herald*'s offices. "But word gets around fast," Vera added. "Barry Greenfield already knew about the event before I told him. Said he's read every Marvel book that's come out, even though he thinks the Percy Bannon series is commercial crap compared to Marvel's first novel, *Weaver's Luck*. He said he's coming an hour early to be sure he gets a seat." Vera chuckled; she hardly ever saw the rabbit *in* a seat. He thought best on his paws.

Just then, Vera spotted a familiar creature coming through the door to the diner. It was the badger Clarence Hobbs. She was about to ask him to join her and Lenore, since she was curious about his job at the mine. But he went directly to a table where a muskrat was already seated and enjoying a plate of cheddar grits.

"Hobbs, there you are!" the muskrat called. "Hoped you could make it. Haven't seen you in months. Bet the mine is keeping you busy. Surprised the boss didn't have you up half the night talking over all the new business."

The badger pulled out a chair and sat, saying, "I'm glad he didn't, because that was the strangest meeting I've ever had with Springfield."

Vera glanced at Lenore, and by silent agreement, the two of them hushed their own conversation and started listening to the badger, though subtly enough that no one else in the diner noticed their interest.

"Never seen the chap in such a state!" Hobbs went on at his friend's urging. "I worry about him, I really do. I'd almost call off my travels, except passage on the ship is already paid for, and my Delia is very keen to visit the family and meet the new nieces and nephews—"

"I'm sure Mr. Springfield would never expect you to give that up, Hobbs!"

"Oh, he didn't say a word about it," Hobbs assured his companion. "I only wondered if it might not be better for the mining operation if I were to stay."

"Take a day to think that over before you scuttle a family trip," the muskrat advised. "You're staying for the funeral, aren't you? Talk to Springfield afterward—he'll be more himself, after the final rites and whatnot."

"Good idea. I sure hope he's feeling better by then. I tell you, he was so distracted, I had to tell him things three times over, and he had to be reminded of stuff *he* taught *me*. He mixed up *feeder* and *footwall* when I was giving him the latest report!"

His friend gaped. "What's more different than those two things? You find one, you maybe got a fresh vein of ore. You find the other, it means the claim's almost done!"

"That's what I'm saying," Hobbs agreed, leaning over the table to pick up a dish of creamer. "The poor sap's all mixed up. I told him the materials arrived for the cribbing, and he just shrugged. As if it didn't matter to him! *He's* the one who made me put the order in last month because the thought of the wall collapsing on the miners kept him up nights."

Lenore gave Vera a quizzical look, but Vera only shook her head. She'd explain the significance of the badger's words later. Right now, her nose was twitching. Hobbs's account was giving her all sorts of ideas.

After signaling Esme and paying their bill, Vera and Lenore

left the diner and walked together a little way down Main Street.

"Well, out with it," Lenore said at last.

Vera quickly looked around to make sure no one was listening. Thankfully, foot traffic was at a lull. "There's something extremely odd going on. Ever since Dorothy claimed Edward was murdered, things have just been . . . askew. Edward is behaving like he's not quite sure what's going to happen next, and I don't just mean following the death of his mother. That was sad but hardly a shock. Edward is acting like he's been . . . stunned. Not to mention I smelled blood on the rug in the Springfields' foyer. Something sinister must have happened there, because if it wasn't sinister, then why did someone cover it up?"

"Well, what are you going to do?"

Vera thought hard about several facts she'd learned in the past few days. The history of the Springfield family; Dorothy's uncertain experience; the quiet, lovely shore of Mirror Lake . . .

"I'm going to talk to Edward again," she declared. "He's hiding something, and I'm going to find out what it is!"

Chapter 6

This time, back in the Springfield house once more, Vera dispensed with the softball questions.

"Mr. Springfield," she said bluntly when they were sitting in the same chairs in the living room, "in all the times I've spoken with you before, about your parents and your family, you never mentioned Thomas. Why is that?"

She'd hoped that, by springing mention of his brother's name on Edward, she would see an unguarded reaction. But Edward only sighed, looking toward the fireplace mantel.

"The less I think about Thomas, the better," he said quietly. "But I suppose you'll need the whole story, or you won't be content."

He paused for a moment, gathering his thoughts. Then

he began, "Thomas is my older brother, and while we were young, I thought the world of him. He was very smart and did the best in all his classes. He was expected to take on the business, of course. And he made time for me, always having fun and playing pranks."

"Sounds like an ideal brother."

"If only it had stayed that way. I think there was something a little off about Thomas. He got into trouble—just small things at first. Pranks that got too mean, like blaming a broken vase on the maids when it was actually Thomas who did it. He didn't always get caught, but when he did, he'd say he was sorry things went wrong and that of course he didn't mean anything by it, but . . ."

"Yes?" Vera prompted.

"Well, the fact is that whether he meant it or not didn't matter. He was hurting folks. He hurt my mother's feelings terribly, not to mention mine. Finally he got into a scrape so bad that there was no apologizing for it. He ran away to escape my father's punishment. And honestly, I never saw him or heard from him again. I know he contacted my parents once or twice. To ask for money, maybe, or just to taunt them. My father wrote him out of the will and the whole mining business, naturally. And he instructed everyone else to ignore any letters Thomas might send. He even ordered several family photographs and paintings to be destroyed because it hurt my mother to see them."

"And Thomas never tried to make your parents change their minds?"

"If he did, I didn't hear of it," Edward explained. "I just tried to live my own life. I had to step up and learn the responsibilities meant for Thomas. As I said, he was older and knew more. I took over a lot of the business after my father passed and more after my mother got sick. She never said Thomas's name again, not even when she knew she didn't have much time left."

"I'm very sorry to bring it up," said Vera, "but I was wondering if it's possible that Thomas came back to Shady Hollow."

"What, now?" Edward looked up, alarm on his features. "Why?"

"Perhaps he finally got word of your father's death or of your mother's illness. Maybe he truly repented his old behavior and wanted to make amends."

"Thomas? Repent?" Edward actually chuckled. "Not a chance. I'm afraid we have to assume that he's unreachable."

"You have no contact information or an address for him?" Vera asked, already knowing what the answer would be.

"Sorry," Edward said, sincerely. "I know he was living in Highbank for a while. But that was years ago. I very much doubt you'd find a trace of him there."

"And he never sent you a single letter?"

He shook his head. "The break was total, and as far as I know I'm the only Springfield son left."

Vera closed her notebook and thanked Edward for his time. He might believe Thomas had vanished off the face of the earth, but Vera knew that folks were rarely so careful. She intended to go to Highbank to discover if her theory could be true.

Returning to Shady Hollow's downtown, Vera noticed some yards were sporting signs that said WE NEED MORE MEADE! in white letters on a bright red background. Very striking. Those signs hadn't been up this morning! Maybe this election would not be the easy victory that she and Orville were hoping for. When she entered the police station, Vera saw that Orville was once more alone in the office. Chief Meade was either fishing or campaigning, or both.

"Hi there," Vera greeted her beau. "Do you have a minute to chat?"

Orville put down the file that he'd been studying and waved her to the chair on the other side of his desk. He knew better than to offer her coffee from the police station's coffeepot. It was notoriously black and noxious, and the carafe was rarely washed.

"What's on your mind?" he asked.

"Um, I happened to speak to Edward Springfield recently, and while I was standing in his foyer, I happened to examine the rug . . ."

"You just happened to examine something in a supposed victim's home?"

"Well, Dot told me she saw blood on the floor. The floor was clean when I saw it, but the rug still has a bloodstain."

"Really? I'll go over there and check it out." He looked pointedly at her. "But in the future, maybe leave the investigations to the police."

"Speaking of that, what happens to police records when you're done with them? You know, like ones from a decade ago?"

Orville frowned thoughtfully. "Well," he began to explain, "at the end of every year, we put the logbooks in a big box and take the box to the storeroom. The logbooks have all the really important entries, like who we arrest and when, and how many calls for help we responded to, and when someone's released and into whose custody and whatnot. But most of the other paperwork gets sent to the village council, and I think they just burn it for fuel in winter."

"Oh, that's all right," she said. "I think arrest records and calls for help would be just what I need."

"This about Dotty?" he asked. "Because I'll tell you right now, she's never been in trouble with the law . . . other than the one time a séance went badly, and in any case the fire brigade declared it an accident."

"No, I'm not concerned about Dorothy Springfield. I want to search for Thomas Springfield."

"Who's that?" Orville asked, puzzled.

"Exactly! Apparently Edward has an older brother named Thomas who's a bad egg. I thought there might be some records of his misdeeds in the police logbooks, even if it's just that he was hauled in for drunkenness one night."

"Hmm. Well, the logbooks are all public. You just need to know what years you want so I can dig the right boxes out of the storeroom."

Vera calculated based on Edward's age and gave Orville a range of five years. He wrote them down, then said, "You'll have to wait a little while for these files, Vera. I've got to complete my shift and then go to the campaign office to see what I need to do there. Folks have been coming in with a lot of questions, some of them pretty tricky. What's my stance on hiring more officers? Will I crack down on those shipments of moonshine that come in from upriver every month? That sort of thing. And Meade started talking about maybe holding a public debate so that voters can hear from the real me . . . whatever that means. I hope I don't have to write a speech. I'd rather answer questions all day!"

"Questions are good," Vera assured him. "The only failing campaign office is an empty campaign office. Please send me a message when you can get those boxes. It's not too urgent . . . just me and one of my wild theories. Anyway, I've got to go and write up this article on Adora along with the obituary. BW wants the whole front page filled so that everyone will go to the funeral and he can get another front page to talk about how many folks showed up."

Afterward, Vera walked to Mr. Fallow's office, where she filled him in on the details she'd managed to uncover. Mr. Fallow nodded along with her report and finally said, "Well, you've done a lot of work in a short amount of time. I'll have to see if any of the Springfield documents even mention Thomas. I have only the vaguest recollection of Edward as a child, seeing as I never would have met with the young ones in the course of business."

"Perhaps Edward would be more forthcoming with you about his brother . . . assuming he'll talk to you at all."

"Oh, I meant to tell you," Mr. Fallow said, smiling at last. "Earlier today, Edward actually stopped by and apologized for his attitude before. He said he's been so torn up about his mother's death and Dot's odd behavior that he lost control of himself entirely. He was ashamed . . . I could see it in his eyes. Said I must do whatever the law dictates is right and that he'll be available to make any statements or give whatever testimony is required. I must say, he sounded so much more like himself. It was quite reassuring."

"I'm glad for that," Vera said. "I wonder if Dorothy might also be feeling a little more like her old self."

"Perhaps we'll find out. Edward said he intends to stop by the bed-and-breakfast in a few days to see if Dot will talk to him. He's so upset about her refusal to accept that he's, well, Edward. He said he'll do it after the funeral. I just hope they can make up again." Mr. Fallow sighed and began to straighten papers on his desk. "After all, nothing happened."

As she left the law office, Vera kept hearing his last words: *nothing happened*. Most folks would agree, because of course Edward was alive and well. But then again, if nothing happened, why was the floor in the hall scrubbed clean and a bloodstained rug placed askew over the spot?

She returned to the newspaper office to complete all the ongoing tasks a reporter has to do. It was a merry-go-round of a job because the moment an issue goes to press, it all starts again for the next issue. Vera worked fast, but it still took a while to plow through the various documents piled in front of her. BW stalked past desks, urging writers to finish pieces and for proofers to hurry, hurry, hurry. He paused at Vera's desk, asking in an arch tone, "Anything actionable today, Vixen?"

"Working on it, BW," she promised, ignoring the sarcasm.

"You'd better be."

As Vera spoke, one of the young hares from the mailroom hurried up to her. "Message from the police station. Deputy Braun wants to see you right away!"

"Thanks!" Vera stood up and grabbed her bag. Orville must have found those logbooks faster than he expected.

When she got to the police station, there was indeed a long box marked with the years Vera had requested. But Orville stood in the middle of the room, a stormy look on his face.

"What's going on, Vera? You pulling a prank on me?"

"Of course not! Why would you even say that?"

"I went to the Springfield house like I said I would. Edward invited me right in, and we talked in the foyer."

"Were you able to examine the crimson rug?" she asked eagerly.

"No, because there was no rug, not of any color. Edward said he'd had a terrible nosebleed a couple nights ago and it stained one corner pretty bad. He tried to clean it but couldn't. So he took it outside and burned it."

"Oh, no! But don't you think that's suspicious?"

"I think it's suspicious that the only creatures talking about blood are dotty Dotty Springfield and you, the reporter who's always chasing a story. There's no evidence of a crime, and poor Edward Springfield is going to bury his mother in a day. And I'm in the middle of a race for my boss's job, so maybe you can just not make my life harder by sending me on a wild-goose chase!"

Vera winced, but protested, "I know what I saw, Orville."

"Not now, Vera." He gestured to the long box. "Here are your musty old records. Take them out of here and have fun reading them, and don't bother me with what you find unless you can back it up with hard evidence. Got it?"

Vera set her jaw and said, "Yes, *Officer*." She grabbed the big box and marched out of the station, steaming mad.

So much for a nice relationship between the media and the law in Shady Hollow!

Chapter 7

On a cool and cloudy day, the townsfolk gathered for Adora Springfield's funeral. The Shady Hollow cemetery was actually a very pretty place, with yew trees surrounding the grounds and many headstones planted with flowers and carefully tended evergreens. Family plots told the history of Shady Hollow's settlement. From the humble graves of sawmill workers to the many, many rows in the Chitters' family plot, nearly everyone living in town could point to a relative several generations before who now slept in the churchyard.

As a recent newcomer, Vera was one of the few who couldn't. Still, she felt a sense of community here among the many creatures who'd gathered and were chatting. They were dressed in black, but the mood was calm. Mrs. Adora Springfield had lived a long and full life. She'd had children and carried on a family business that was known throughout the region. In the end, she was at peace. There was little to be sad about in that.

Lenore, who always dressed in black, stepped up to Vera. "Quite the crowd, hmm? Have you seen the Springfield crypt yet?"

"No, I thought I'd wait for locals to pay their respects first."

"Then you'll be waiting until next winter. Come on, it's quite a sight."

Lenore led Vera up a slope.

Several families had crypts, and they were all arranged around this hill, dug deep into the side of it to take advantage of the natural feature. But very few crypts stood on top, and the Springfields' was at the highest point. Vera was impressed by the gracious architecture: each corner of the elegant gray stone skillfully carved to resemble tree trunks, wildflowers etched along the sides, a fountain sculpted in relief. The words NO MATTER HOW COLD THE WINTER, SPRING ALWAYS RETURNS were engraved above the fountain. Vera tipped her head, seeing a silvery gleam in the design.

"Yup," Lenore whispered. "Your eyes are not playing tricks on you. There's real silver on those walls. The Springfield mining operation does very good business, and the family pays for someone to come here and polish the silver insets to keep the tarnish off. They've got enough money to have maid service for the dead. Now *that's* a power move."

Vera nodded, unable to come up with a clever rejoinder in the face of this revelation. She also felt another twinge of worry. If her time as a journalist had taught her anything, it was that money is responsible for a lot of evil deeds. If the Springfield fortune was so large, maybe someone would kill for it. Or *say* that someone was killed . . .

She shook her head. It was useless to speculate on Dorothy's strange declaration that her husband had died despite him standing there. What possible motive would she have to make such an announcement? After all, Dorothy was now out of the inheritance, based on the summary of the will that Mr. Fallow had given Vera. If anything, Dorothy should want to insist Edward was alive even if he wasn't.

Vera spotted Orville not too far away, standing awkwardly near a tall stone grave. He caught her gaze and seemed about to walk over, but she quickly turned away. She wasn't ready to speak to Orville yet.

"You all right?" Lenore asked.

"Oh, nothing. Orville and I had a little argument yesterday. He doesn't want to hear about the Springfield case."

"There is no Springfield case," Lenore reminded her.

"I'm not so sure." Vera informed her friend about the disappearance of the bloodstained rug.

"Huh. Circumstantial at best," Lenore said. (She was an avid reader of true crime.)

"Looks like Dorothy isn't talking to Edward, either." Vera sighed when she noticed each Springfield standing far away from the other.

"Maybe she'll come around in a little while. Edward has tried to visit her at the B and B, you know. Very polite, as always. Comes to the door every day and asks Ben if he can speak to Dot. And poor Ben always has to say no. But Edward brings a bouquet and Ben takes it on Dotty's behalf. It's really rather tragic," Lenore added in a rush.

Vera nodded. She couldn't argue. Ravens are the experts on tragedy.

A podium had been set up at the base of the hill, and this was where the family gathered around the closed coffin. Parson James "Dusty" Conkers stood near the podium, patiently waiting to begin the service.

"I think we should go find our places," Vera murmured to her friend. "No one likes funerals to begin late."

"The deceased might want to put them off," the raven countered, deadpan.

Dusty delivered a beautiful sermon. The jackrabbit possessed a resonant voice that could project for a quarter mile (a skill developed when he was a circuit minister on the western prairies). He spoke of Adora's deep love for her family and her neighbors. He told of Adora's unfailing generosity, such as when a thunderstorm had swept through Mirror Lake and she'd housed thirteen families in her own home for a week until repairs could be made to the damaged buildings. A huge oak tree had fallen and blocked her own front door, so she'd simply had everyone use the storm door to the basement instead!

After the service, Vera and Lenore encountered the von Beaverpelts, who'd been standing nearby.

Edith von Beaverpelt looked around. "Mrs. Springfield must have been quite a personality. Such a lot of folks have come!"

"I'm sure more came to Daddy's funeral," Stasia said quickly.

"If that's even true, it was only for the spectacle," Esme countered. "No one can say our father was particularly loved."

"Oh, what a thing to say!" Edith lifted a lacy pawkerchief to her nose and sniffed. She did not, however, deny the statement.

"The wake is at the family home," Lenore noted. "Will you all be attending?"

"Well, sure, but this wake probably won't be as fancy as Daddy's," Stasia said.

"Yeah, it probably won't be as dramatic, either," Esme added. "Remember when his *mistress* showed up and started shouting?"

Edith moaned and swayed as if she were about to faint. "Must I never forget that moment?" she wailed. "So ungracious . . ."

Vera helped her to a stone bench even though she suspected Edith was just being dramatic. The crowd had broken up, and creatures had begun chatting with one another in low voices, many of them preparing to make the slow, solemn walk to the Springfield house to join the wake.

Just then, Edward approached Dot, clearly wanting to restore their relationship. "Dot, you planned so much of this service, and it all turned out so well."

Dot, who was standing with Ben and Geoffrey Eastwood, looked slightly mollified but said only, "It's the least I could do for Adora."

"You did so much more for Mother, and I'll always be grateful you were there for her at the end. Oh, darling, please can't we make up? On this day of all days. My mother laid in the ground. Can't we be together again, like we were? I hate this . . . you so distraught and not even sleeping in our house but at an inn!"

Dot seemed to waver, saying in a low voice, "How's the house? At sixes and sevens, I'll bet. Not even swept for weeks . . ."

"It's fine, Dotty. It's just fine. Let's go back there now and sort everything out. Please, my sweet Dotty."

Suddenly Dot narrowed her eyes and stepped back. "No! I cannot do that. No, don't move an inch closer!"

Ben, though far smaller than Edward, moved between the

couple. "Perhaps it would be best if I escort Mrs. Springfield back to the B and B. She ought to rest."

Edward's jaw had gone tight, and Vera sensed the almost-electric charge of an animal ready to spring into battle.

Before Edward could make a move, Orville was there, his bulk huge and uncompromising.

"That's a good idea, Ben. Take Dot back, would you? I'll swing by in a little while to make sure everyone's settled."

It was a politely worded warning, but a warning all the same. Edward would find stiff resistance if he tried to enter Bramblebriar Inn today.

Edward's stance relaxed into compliance. "A difficult day for everyone," he said, nodding. "I'll just go back to the house and see that everything is in order for the wake. All are welcome, of course. I hope to see everyone there." He looked appealingly at Dorothy as he said the last words, but she refused to meet his gaze.

"Well," Esme muttered to Vera, "scratch what I said about not being so dramatic. I say, Shady Hollow sure knows how to do a funeral."

Chapter 8

Ben was helping Dot walk back to the inn after the funeral and the incident with Edward. Vera came to support Dorothy's other side, since it looked as if she might faint at any minute. The rat was mumbling under her breath.

"Did you hear what he called me? He *never* calls me Dotty, never!"

Vera overheard this. "What do you mean he never calls you Dotty?" she asked in a soothing tone, not wanting to upset Dot further.

Dot stopped whispering and stared at Vera.

"Why, Edward never called me Dotty," she said, as if surprised that this was not common knowledge. "He always called me Doro. It was his pet name for me."

Vera took this in and pondered what it could mean. Was it possible that Edward was so upset over losing his mother and fighting with his wife that he'd simply forgot to use the special name that he had used every day of their married life? An idea began to form in her brain, and she wanted to be alone to examine it further. Once Vera got Dot comfortably settled at the bed-and-breakfast, she would head home and let her little gray cells do some work.

Ben opened the gate to the yard of the inn, and Vera put a paw on Dot's shoulder to guide her down the gravel path. "Just a few more steps now, Dot," she said, keeping her tone low.

Then Dot's eyes widened and she squeaked in fear. "What . . . what's that?"

Vera looked to where the rat was pointing. A huge shadow loomed against the wall of the inn! Before Vera could determine any more about it, the shadow suddenly moved, and a dark shape emerged into the fading light of the day. Black fabric fluttered around the shape, and something concealed the features of the face, hooding it in mystery.

Vera felt a deep instinct to flee—an emotion so primal that all the civilization in the world can't eradicate it from a creature's psyche. It was fear, raw fear. The fear that prey feels when confronted by a predator. What horrible being had come to haunt Dorothy Springfield on the very day of the funeral that laid Adora to rest?

Then the shape spoke. "Hello, friends."

The figure raised a paw and lifted the wide brim of a fedora to reveal a wolfish countenance and flashing sharp white teeth. He then allowed his black trench coat to flap open in the breeze. Underneath it he wore a well-tailored maroon suit. "I do hope this is the right place."

"Mr. Marvel, I presume," Geoffrey Eastwood said, all at once recovering from his own fright. He was again the friendly innkeeper ready to receive a guest. "Come inside, sir, and I'll get you registered and settled. Ben will grab your bags in a moment. He and Vera are just helping our other guest upstairs."

Vera glanced at Bradley Marvel as she passed him on the porch. He was a handsome creature, no doubt.

He flashed a grin at Vera and said, "This town looks better every moment."

After seeing that Dot was settled in her room and that no unwanted visitors would enter, Vera returned to the porch. She stood in silence for a moment, thinking that she ought to head to her den to prepare for the next event. Most folks would head for the wake shortly after darkness fell. (Long-standing rat etiquette dictates that while burials ought to take place *before* sundown, wakes ought not to start until *after* sundown.)

Before Vera could step off the porch, she heard a voice say, "I seem to have arrived at an inopportune time." There was Bradley Marvel again. He looked quite comfortable sitting on one of the brightly painted rocking chairs.

"Yes, we had a funeral today," Vera explained.

"So sorry," he said in a tone that did not seem very sorry. "I don't suppose you might show me around town? What's your name?"

"Vera Vixen. I'm a reporter with the Shady Hollow *Herald*."

"A reporter! Well, well. You must know your way around. Where's this Nevertheless Books?"

"It's called Nevermore Books, and I'll be happy to show you the way," she said, even though it would make her late for the wake. "Lenore is so excited to hold the event tomorrow night. We expect a big crowd for it."

Bradley stood up and adjusted his fedora to a more rakish angle. "Let us advance! Always ready to meet the little folks who make my career possible."

Vera let that remark pass by without comment and instead asked about his trip. "Didn't run into any problems, I hope. The boat service is reliable, except during winter."

"Ha! Nothing like the wild river of Amazonia, where I went to research my third book. Now *that's* a river journey to remember. Deadly whirlpools and poisonous plants and thunderstorms mornings and evenings. But I'm more interested in this 'not quite a murder' thing I just heard about. Can it really be that the poor lady thinks her husband is dead in spite of him walking around and talking to her?"

"Dorothy Springfield is quite certain that her husband is dead and that the rat everyone sees is some sort of . . . impostor, I suppose. It's quite distressing." Vera didn't add that she was investigating the case. Bradley Marvel sounded interested, but he was a stranger in town. *Huh,* she thought, *look at me, thinking like a born-and-bred local after just a few years.*

Vera continued, "The fact is that Dot made her accusation the day after her mother-in-law died and she had to travel all the way back home. That would put anyone out of sorts."

"'Out of sorts' means you snap at the neighbors and skip weeding the flower bed for a few days. Telling your husband he's dead is something else entirely. And no one's been able to convince her that she's wrong?" Marvel pressed.

"Not yet. If you've got any tips, I'd be glad to hear them."

"Well, I'm not a psychologist, but I've picked up a thing or two," he replied. "Sounds to me like she needs an intervention . . . her husband and her friends and her neighbors to all sit her down and tell her what's what until she admits she made a mistake."

"Sounds drastic," Vera murmured.

They'd just entered Nevermore Books when Vera heard a loud gasp. Then a sheep trotted up to Marvel, glaring at the writer. "You!" she declared.

"Yes, that's what I assumed, ma'am," Bradley said, nonplussed by the sudden approach. "Care for a signature?"

Instead, the sheep tossed a copy of his novel onto the floor. "I do *not* care for a signature! You were supposed to come here on tour before now. I waited all day to see the great Bradley Marvel, only to find that the event was canceled without warning! I'll never read your books again. I bet they're all terrible now anyway."

Just as swiftly as she'd appeared, the sheep stormed off like a fluffy low-flying cloud of crackling rage. Vera half expected to see lightning bolts strike passersby.

Embarrassed on behalf of the town, Vera said, "Ah, sorry about that. She must have been a passionate fan to be so upset. I assure you that the Hollow's residents are much more polite than that example."

"Ah, I won't lose sleep over it," Marvel said. "Comes with the job."

"She shouldn't have said that—about your books being horrible, I mean. I'm sure they're fantastic." Vera had read only a few and had not found them fantastic, but she was too discreet to say so.

At this awkward moment, Vera had run out of polite chitchat and was relieved to see Lenore wing her way down from an upper level of the bookshop. Lenore landed near her friend and waited. Bradley Marvel was looking expectant. Vera realized it was up to her to make introductions.

"Mr. Marvel," Vera began politely, "this is Lenore Lee, the owner of Nevermore Books. And Lenore," she continued, "this is Bradley Marvel, the author."

The two creatures nodded at each other, and then Lenore took charge. "It's such an honor to have you here in my shop, Mr. Marvel," Lenore said smoothly. "We're all set for your event tomorrow evening. Won't you come with me?"

Lenore had dealt with many authors, from beginners to the truly famous, and she treated them all with the same courtesy. Even if she hated a particular writer's latest novel, one would never know it from her demeanor. Lenore glanced over to where the cash register was located and saw a young mouse hovering nervously. The entire Chitters clan was extremely hardworking, and Lenore had been happy to hire Violet Chitters to help out in the bookshop part-time. The young mouse was a voracious reader and a huge fan of Bradley Marvel. Lenore gestured to her employee, and Violet came closer, staring at the ground.

"Mr. Marvel," Lenore began the introduction, "this is Violet, my assistant. She can help with whatever you might require."

"Hello there, young lady," Bradley Marvel said brightly. He could not be bothered with remembering the names of shop assistants. Lenore realized this, but Violet did not.

"Oh, Mr. Marvel," the young mouse gushed, "I'm so excited to meet you! I've read all your books!"

"That's terrific," the great wolf responded, looking over the mouse's head to see who was listening.

Violet was far too nervous to continue speaking to her

idol. Lenore stepped in and suggested that Bradley start pre-
signing the stock so he wouldn't have to sign so many tomorrow. This was something that authors often did at large events.
He could quickly sign all the books and then, after the event, he
could personalize them for his fans. This saved a great deal of
time as well as stress on the author's paw. Lenore indicated a
table where piles of Marvel's latest novel were stacked. There
was also a book cart completely filled with the new title.
Nevermore Books was expecting a record crowd, and Lenore
had ordered with abandon. She was counting on these book
sales to get her through until the holidays.

The author settled himself at the table and browsed the
selection of pens that had been set out for his use. Vera watched
Violet stand at his side and begin flapping the books. Violet
opened each book to the title page, where Bradley Marvel was
to sign, and placed the front flap of the book jacket over the
pages. This way each book could be quickly and easily opened
to the title page. This little method streamlined the signing
process. It also helped Violet relax by giving her something to
do with her paws while so close to her idol.

Bradley Marvel began to scrawl his signature on the many
copies of his new book. Violet and Lenore worked quietly
and efficiently beside him. Violet passed Bradley a book open
to the title page, he scribbled his signature, and then Lenore
removed the book and placed it on an empty book cart.
This was repeated again and again. The author began to
regale his companions with stories about his many research
trips and adventures around the globe. Lenore was listening
politely, but Violet was enraptured. She was too nervous to
say anything, so Bradley Marvel had the floor. At one point
he got thirsty and asked for a beverage. Vera took this as

an opportunity to escape the bookstore and volunteered to fetch one.

The author asked for a cappuccino, and Vera left for the coffee shop with a sigh of relief. How that wolf could talk about himself!

Joe's Mug was relatively quiet when Vera entered. She waved a paw at Esme, who was refilling mugs for a few customers. Then Vera went to the counter and said hello to Joe.

"How are you, Vera?" asked the moose. "I hear Orville's campaign is going well."

"I hope so," she replied, not adding that she'd had a spat with Orville and thus was not up to date on the news. "But now I'm here to get coffee for our famous author. He wants a cappuccino. Can you throw in some of those cranberry-orange muffins? I'm getting hungry, and the folks at the bookshop probably want a snack, too."

Joe said no more but whipped up a cappuccino and put some muffins in a bag. Vera paid him and turned to go. She planned to drop off the coffee and the treats and then get back to her investigation.

Before Vera reached the diner door, none other than Professor Heidegger entered. The owl had attended the funeral earlier, like nearly all the Hollow's citizens, but Vera hadn't got a chance to speak to him.

"How are you, Professor?" Vera asked politely.

He blinked his large eyes and said, "Enervated, Miss Vixen. I am not, as you know, typically diurnal, but needs must. One must show respect for tradition, and Adora Springfield would have done the same for me, I trust. We matriculated from the same college, you know. Fine creature, decorous and exemplary in all ways."

"It was good of you to attend the funeral," Vera said, "and lucky you returned from visiting your cousins in time. I heard there was some, er, confusion at your house when you got back?"

"No confusion at all, Miss Vixen. Some scamp, some squatter, some miscreant had enjoyed my domicile without permission while I was in absentia! Very rude, I say. There is a fine inn for guests in town, not to mention rooms to let for those of lesser means and the woods if one is destitute. To commandeer my home is most uncalled for!" His feathers had puffed out so much during this indignant speech that he resembled a dandelion about to burst apart.

"But nothing was stolen?" she asked.

Heidegger hooted in annoyance. "Nothing of value, though my larder was considerably depleted by the unwelcome guest. And the books all read through and reshelved in the wrong places! I suspect my collection of local yearbooks may take years to put back together. I have a more-complete collection than the library's, you know. Some of the pages had been dog-eared!"

"Oh, no!" Vera gasped in horror; Heidegger clearly expected this offense to bring the most outrage. In truth, she had been known to fold over the corner of a page or two when a bookmark could not be located.

"True! And the police insist they can do nothing because I cannot prove that these crimes were committed by someone other than me."

"I'm so sorry to hear all that, Professor. Perhaps you can search your house until you find some evidence that will support your claim."

"Oh, I looked," he said, "but whoever it was left nothing

behind. And Deputy Braun won't listen to me when I tell him that I never shelved *Shady Hollow: A History* next to *The Flavors of the Forest*. Entirely different genres!" He flapped both wings wide with indignation. "So I am deserted in my time of need, and I'll have to re-sort all the books myself, which will probably take until next spring. Meanwhile, the miscreant is probably skipping off to the next town to steal someone else's maple-roasted nut mix purchased specially from the Ms. Muncie's Munchies catalog. It has cashews in it!"

"Oh, that's a real tragedy," Vera said with sincerity (one never wants to have one's favorite snack stolen). "But since you've mentioned it, I wonder if I might stop by tomorrow to look at your books. I'm researching a story, and I've come up short with the public collections. And you've got so many unique books."

"Certainly, my dear lady!" he responded, perking up at the compliment. "Midafternoon would be best. I'll be sure to wake early for your visit."

Vera thanked him and promised she'd ring loudly when she arrived the next day. "Now if you'll excuse me, I need to drop off this coffee and then get ready for Adora's wake."

Chapter 9

Vera dressed in a black velvet gown for the wake, draping a cloak over herself for warmth, as the evening had turned quite brisk. A wind had sprung up from the north, reminding anyone walking that evening that winter was on its way.

Vera met up with Lenore, and the two friends walked to Mirror Lake, chatting as they went. The raven's mind was fully occupied with the event she would be holding at the bookstore in less than twenty-four hours' time, and Vera wanted to relieve her of as much stress as she could. That's what friends do.

Before they knew it, they'd arrived. The wake for Adora Springfield was held at the original family home, the very house where Dorothy made her drastic accusation and where Edward now lived alone, suffering from both his mother's death and his wife's absence. Naturally, Dorothy did not make an appearance all night. But many other creatures did.

Vera and Lenore joined the line of folks entering the house, many of whom were bearing little bouquets of flowers or letters of condolence or small gifts.

Edward stood at the door, greeting each and every creature as they came in. He was somberly dressed in a black suit with a yellow carnation blossom in a tiny silver boutonniere vase pinned to his lapel. He nodded and spoke to everyone for a moment, then invited them to partake of the food and drink inside and to share their memories of Adora.

Vera listened to Lenore's event preparations with one ear and to the buzz of conversation around her with the other. As Vera and Lenore approached the doorway, the fox overheard Edward just ahead of them. He was talking to a guest who'd brought a bottle of port bedecked with a ribbon.

"Stanley Mortimer, you shouldn't have," Edward said, but he chuckled. "That is not to say I won't drink it. How long has it been since I've seen you?"

"Must have been that dinner in August, eh?" the rat answered.

"Feels like much longer than that. We've got to have another dinner soon, Stan. Please go in, make yourself at home. Thank you for coming, friend."

"You know I'd never let you down, Ed," Stan responded. "Anything you need, you say the word."

Edward nodded gratefully and turned to the next guests, who happened to be Vera and Lenore.

"Miss Vixen," he said, "what a wonderful piece you wrote

in the paper about my mother. I think you really captured her life in a way few others could."

"I'm glad to hear it, Mr. Springfield." In truth, Vera thought he'd been a bit annoyed with her when they last spoke. *He simply must be under stress.* "Your stories were so much help in writing it."

Edward smiled sadly. "Stories are all I have left. But please, ladies, come in, come in. Coatrack is at the end of the foyer, and you'll find food and drink in the large parlor. I'm so overwhelmed by how many folks have come."

They passed into the house, which was indeed getting crowded already. Vera instinctively looked at the floor and saw that an entirely new rug covered it, this one in a midnight hue. "Hmm," she said softly. "That's different."

"The rug?" Lenore asked. "It's a rat thing. They claim floorcloths are a very practical method to prevent damaging and dirtying floors during large events. The color shouldn't matter, but for funerals and wakes and whatnot, they're always black, or dark-colored if you can't get black on short notice. I tell you, rats can claim they're not superstitious, but no rat will have a pink floorcloth at a funeral!"

"You're a font of information," Vera told her friend.

"I took a class at university all about rituals of death among various species."

"Of course you did," Vera murmured.

They helped themselves to wine and chatted with the other guests. Vera probed gently for opinions on the incident with Dorothy, and the consensus seemed to be that Dotty just needed some time to relax and that Edward would be able to talk her back to sense in a week or so.

"Such a couple, you know," one slightly tipsy rat confided

to Vera. "They got married practically the first day they legally could. For the school yearbook we voted them the couple most likely to stick together forever."

"I hope you turn out to be right," Vera said. But no longer was she focused on the case of Dorothy Springfield—she'd seen a bear across the room.

Orville.

At the funeral earlier, she'd ignored him, not ready to get into yet another fight about whether she was right or wrong to pursue an investigation on her own. But now, having heard about Edward and Dot's lifelong love story, she wondered if she was only hurting herself by avoiding Orville.

He caught her gaze, and she nodded cautiously. He took that as a cue to come over, parting the crowd as he did so thanks to his sheer size. However, he did get stopped several times as folks shook his paw or spoke to him, presumably about the election. He chatted and shook paws and nodded, but he continued to make his way toward Vera.

"I'm gone," whispered Lenore, who promptly faded into the crowd.

Then Orville was standing in front of Vera, neither of them speaking.

"You look very nice tonight," Orville said at last.

"Thank you." Vera wanted to say that the bear looked quite well turned out himself, but the words that emerged were "Let's stop fighting."

"That's a *great* idea," he agreed with a relieved exhale. "There's nothing like attending a wake alone to remind you of how much there is to lose."

"I get that. I mean, I came here with Lenore, so I wasn't alone. But I *was* . . . except now I'm not." She reached out a paw and touched his sleeve. "You know, it's a little stuffy in here. How would you feel about a walk along the lake?"

He smiled. "Fine idea, Miss Vixen. Meet me at the door, and we'll get out of here."

And that is what they did.

───────

The day after the wake, Vera wrote a short article about the event, avoided BW's questions about whether Dotty was seeing ghosts, and dashed out to Joe's for a coffee, all before her visit to Professor Heidegger's in the afternoon. Before leaving for her appointment with the professor, Vera bought a treat from Joe's bakery display case—a sticky nut roll, the kind of which she knew the professor was especially fond.

At the base of the great elm tree that Heidegger called home, Vera pulled the bell rope to alert the owl. In response, a basket attached to a thin rope dropped from above. A moment later, a more substantial rope ladder tumbled down as well.

"Put your things in the basket and then climb up!" the owl called. "I shall handle the rest. I have a very precise system in place."

Vera deposited the bakery bag and the coffee in the basket and slung her own pack around her shoulders. She climbed nimbly up the ladder and soon arrived at the top, which ended on a branch broad enough for dancing. Heidegger was a few feet away, turning a crank that winched up the basket.

"Good afternoon, Miss Vixen," he said. "I trust the libations of the previous evening did you no ill. Adora would have enjoyed her wake, I must say."

"It was quite the event," Vera agreed, watching as the basket came into view. She leaned over to pluck out the bakery bag and her coffee (which was still upright; the basket had several loops designed to hold fragile items). "I brought you a sticky nut roll just in case you needed a snack."

"Ooooh, delightful!" Heidegger hooted. "And much needed, for I've not yet been able to get my marketing done and my larder is shockingly destitute."

"About that," Vera said as the owl ushered her into his home, "I wanted to ask if you were able to learn any more about the creature who apparently broke in a couple weeks ago."

Heidegger gave another hoot, this time in indignation. "Alas, no. But I have now compiled a list of items missing from my home." He grabbed a long sheet of paper and began to recite:

> *Cookies (chocolate)*
> *Books (twenty-three)*
> *Nut mix (one can, Ms. Muncie's brand)*
> *Peanut butter (one jar, same brand)*
> *Multiple pages from Shady Hollow's*
>   *Neighborhoods scrapbook (torn out)*
> *Pencils (seven)*

"You know how many pencils you own?" Vera interrupted.

"Of course! One must keep accounts accurate. That's why I was so annoyed at Deputy Braun. He thinks I'm scatterbrained with my head in the clouds, but I do know what I'm about."

"Tell me more about the books that went missing," she said. "I wonder if we can find a pattern." (She did not care in the least about the food or the sundries. Pencil thievery just didn't seem like a threat.)

"Ah, yes. Please have a look."

He led her to his bookcases, which went from floor to ceiling since he could easily fly up to fetch a title. Some books leaned over on the shelves, and there were many gaps in the arrangement, but the owl jabbed an accusing wing toward very particular openings. "See here? That was my annotated copy of *Shady Hollow: A History*. And here—a very rare first edition of *The Flavors of the Forest*. It's one of the seminal woodland cookbooks. Even my Shady Hollow street directory was stolen, and it was this year's edition!" He pointed to a mostly empty shelf then. "And there—nearly a decade's worth of yearbooks from the local schools."

"But surely many creatures have copies," Vera said. "Every student from each year, to start!" She was puzzled over the loss of such mundane items.

"It's not that they're rare; it's that they're useful, you know. I can't tell you how often I've gone to a yearbook to confirm a spelling or to find out that a creature spent a year abroad or what have you."

"I see," she said. "What else went missing? You said some pages were ripped out of books."

"Indeed." He shuddered at the barbarism of it. "The thief must have been utterly mad because there's no rhyme or reason to such an act. It appears they detested beauty. They ripped out several illustrations and maps but also random pages from local histories. I tell you, Miss Vixen, it was the product of unbounded rage. I only wish I had arrived home in time to confront the criminal!"

"Be glad you didn't," Vera said. "If they're as dangerous as you suppose, you might have been hurt . . . or worse."

"Never!" Heidegger declared. "This is a civilized world."

Vera did not respond to that but instead tried a different topic. "Well, thank you for speaking with me. And now you must excuse me. I didn't realize the time. I've got to get to the bookstore soon! Are you coming? Tonight's event with Bradley Marvel is going to draw the biggest crowd in years."

"Huh!" Heidegger said. "That sort of thing is a little too accessible for a scholar such as myself. I shall be at home reading a more enlightening selection by the fire."

Vera made sympathetic noises while searching for an escape route. Heidegger was in general a good sort, but he tended to think the world began and ended with him. While Vera always wanted to get a scoop, the theft of books and pencils and peanut butter didn't sound like much of a lead, and it was almost time for the book signing!

Chapter 10

From Professor Heidegger's, Vera hurried home to change into a new outfit. She wanted to be comfortable enough to help Lenore move chairs but to still appear stylish for a date with Orville. She was going to the bookshop a little early to help with any last-minute preparations that might be needed and had told Orville to meet her there.

The weather forecast predicted a clear and crisp autumn evening, which was fortunate. Whenever the weather was bad, the residents of Shady Hollow tended to stay in their various cozy houses, cottages, and dens.

When Vera arrived at Nevermore Books, it appeared Lenore had the situation under control. Rows of colorful folding chairs were set up to face the podium where Bradley Marvel would speak. A glass of water was at the ready. Lenore flitted around, making sure the trays of hors d'oeuvres were in place along with the glasses and the wine.

The store was starting to fill as most of the residents of Shady Hollow gathered for what might prove to be the literary event of the year. Vera chose two empty seats in the next-to-last row. The fox knew Orville was on his way, but if he were delayed for any reason, he would be able to slip in without making a fuss. After Vera took her seat and nodded to a few neighbors, she looked around the store. There was a poster of the author at the front and a large blowup of the cover of his new book. Vera studied the photo of Marvel and had to admit he was quite handsome. Perhaps she'd judged him too quickly before, and he was more skilled at writing than at social niceties. Clearly his publisher supported him well.

Vera saw Chief Meade enter the bookstore. He was chatting and shaking paws with various creatures, clapping others on the back with a friendly wink, or doffing his hat to the ladies. Though Meade was known to be a bit of a slacker when it came to actually working, he was well aware of how to present himself as a reliable, useful figure whom folks could trust. There was a reason he'd been chief for so long.

Vera knew Meade was campaigning hard, so she hoped Orville would show up soon to provide a counterbalance. Vera no sooner had this thought when she felt a large presence on her left as Orville dropped into the seat that she had saved for him. He gave her a quick kiss on the cheek.

"Quite a crowd," he observed. Orville was not a big reader, but even he was familiar with the works of Bradley Marvel; he liked to point out any mistakes in police procedure that occurred in the books.

Vera enjoyed the cheerful babble of many creatures all talking at once and the excitement in the air. Lenore appeared at the podium, hovering briefly and then perching on the edge. A hush fell over the crowd.

"I'd like to welcome you all to Nevermore Books," she said. "We have quite a treat for you tonight: the acclaimed author of the well-known Percy Bannon series. I am proud to present for the first time in Shady Hollow . . . Bradley Marvel!"

There was an eruption of applause and a few wolf whistles, and then the extremely dapper gray wolf came out from the back room and approached the podium. Lenore flew out of the way and took a place at the back of the crowd where she could watch the event.

"Thanks so much, Lee Anne," the wolf said smoothly. "It's such an honor to be here tonight. I'm just going to read a little bit from my new book, *Hard Pass*, and then I'll take a few questions before signing. As I'm sure you all know, this is the ninth book in the Percy Bannon series." A cheer went up from a group of squirrels in the front.

Vera struggled not to roll her eyes. How had she ever thought that this pompous ass was handsome? He couldn't even get Lenore's name right. She hoped the raven hadn't noticed (though Vera was certain she had).

As the wolf began to read in a rather affected tone, Vera tuned him out and looked around at the crowd instead. She was surprised to spot Professor Heidegger at the back of the room. His mere presence was startling enough, but Vera was even more shocked to observe that he was accompanied by a squirrel, who was pulling a red wagon absolutely filled with books. Vera narrowed her eyes when she saw that all the books in the wagon were Bradley Marvel titles.

"'Too accessible,' huh?" Vera murmured. The professor must've been a superfan of the author! He'd hired the squirrel to pull the wagon. It appeared quite heavy, and Heidegger was known for his intellect, not his muscle. Vera smiled to herself. Ambrosius Heidegger was a bit of a know-it-all, and he spoke of only highbrow subjects. It amused the fox to think that the owl shared this interest with so many others in town.

After what seemed like an incredibly long time to Vera but was really only about twenty minutes, Marvel concluded his recitation. There was a round of applause from the audience, and then the author began to take questions. Vera tuned out again and thought about Dot. She knew there was something very strange about Dot's situation and her refusal to believe that Edward was Edward, but Vera still needed more facts about the Springfield family.

When the questions had dwindled down to a very persistent chipmunk wanting to know where Bradley Marvel had purchased his fedora, Lenore flew up to the podium to end the Q-and-A section of the evening. She assured her customers that books were available for sale at the front desk and that Bradley Marvel had signed every single one but would personalize copies now. There was a rush to the signing table since many of the attendees had already purchased their books. Folks jostled and mumbled; everyone wanted to be the first in line to meet the idol. However, Vera noticed that Professor Heidegger had chosen a different tactic—he and his wagon were waiting patiently at the end of the queue.

Things progressed smoothly. Lenore was selling books at the front desk at a steady clip. The atmosphere in the bookshop was almost like a holiday. Vera would be surprised if the other businesses in town had any customers. It truly seemed as if every resident of Shady Hollow were present at the reading this evening.

"It would be great if Lenore could host more events like this. Then she wouldn't have to work so hard," Vera said to Barry Greenfield, who was standing nearby clutching his first-edition copy of *Weaver's Luck*.

Then Vera caught sight of a commotion at the front of the store. A deer had entered Nevermore Books. She was standing at the edge of the crowd, as if searching for someone, and casting her head around in a distracted manner that was not at all like the cheerful moods of the other customers.

Vera frowned, trying to remember the doe's name. *Cassie? Cassia! That's it. Cassia Brocket.*

"Something's wrong," Vera murmured to Barry.

"Definitely," he replied. Both were lifelong reporters, and they could sense the change in the air.

Vera watched with concern as Cassia spotted Orville chatting with some neighbors and then headed right for him. Police bears do tend to stand out in a crowd.

Vera made her way through the throng just in time to hear the deer say in a low, urgent tone, "You've got to come right away, Officer! I found a dead body in the woods!"

Chapter 11

There was a collective gasp from the creatures near enough to overhear Cassia Brocket's announcement. Orville did not want to make a scene, so he shushed the deer and drew her into a corner to ask some questions.

A short while later, a small group of creatures led by Orville, who carried a lantern, left the bookstore as quietly as possible, though whispers were already spreading among the gathered attendees. Vera sent Lenore an apologetic glance—how vexing to have the biggest event of the year end like this!—but she also wanted to get to the crime scene as fast as she could, and she was grateful that Orville hadn't told her to skedaddle. In the past, she'd often argued with him over the rights of the press versus the protocols of police investigation, and they still didn't always see eye to eye on it.

But now Orville seemed wholly focused on discovering exactly what Ms. Brocket had found and if it was indeed linked to Dot Springfield's accusation of murder.

"Are folks still looking for treasure out here?" Orville asked when they reached the patch of woods in question. "I thought that nonsense was forgotten by now."

"Clearly not by everyone," Vera said quietly. "A lot of folks think there's a cache of precious gemstones buried in these woods. Buried by . . . well, you know . . ." Vera didn't like to think of the first murder she'd covered as a reporter for the *Herald*. It had happened not long ago, and the killer had boasted of hiding getaway money in the forest outside town. The rumor persisted among the residents. Most discounted the possibility, but there was enough danger and romance in the rumors that folks would take excursions to dig randomly in the hopes of striking it rich.

Ms. Brocket certainly wasn't one of the creatures doing the digging. She'd just had the bad luck of coming across an opened grave, the contents of which must have caused the original searchers to flee the scene . . . because sticking out of the dirt was the unmistakable shape of a creature's paw.

"Well, hell," Orville said, staring down at the grave. "This is going to make for a long night."

"Maybe the body is old," Ms. Brocket offered hopefully. "Maybe it's not a murder victim at all but just a creature who died long ago and was buried way out . . . here . . ." She trailed off. There was no reason for a creature to be disposed of in such a manner.

"It's not old," Orville countered. "Not with that smell."

Vera had to agree, for the odor of decay suggested a very recent death. "It's wrapped in something. A bedsheet maybe. We'll need shovels to get the body all the way out so it can be examined. And look—the ground here is disturbed. If this were an old grave, the soil would be packed down from weather and rain and time, except for in places where the shovel turned it over. But this dirt is loose and soft. It was dug up and turned not long ago, *before* the treasure hunters came."

Orville pawed at the ground, grunting in agreement. "We'll have to send for Dr. Broadhead," he said. "He'll be able to tell us more about the creature and the time and cause of death."

"Oh, how horrible," Ms. Brocket was saying, turning her head away. "Some poor creature . . ."

"Sorry you were the one to discover it, ma'am," Orville said gruffly, "but you did the right thing by telling the police immediately. Now why don't you go on home for the night? If I've got any more questions for you, I'll stop by tomorrow and ask."

"Thanks, Deputy Braun," Ms. Brocket said, obviously happy to be leaving the grisly scene.

Vera cleared her throat then, the sound coming out very much like *"cough-fidential."*

"Oh, right," Orville said. "And I must ask you, Ms. Brocket, not to tell anyone the details of this scene until I or Chief Meade say it's okay. In the interests of justice, and for the sake of this creature's family, we don't want to say too much before we've got all the facts."

The doe nodded, her eyes big and serious. Vera suspected that she'd pour out at least part of the story to all and sundry, but then again, there weren't many details to reveal at the moment. For example, they couldn't even be sure of the victim's species. Orville found a discarded shovel nearby and began using it to expose more of the body in the grave.

The moment Cassia Brocket left, another creature arrived. Vera looked over her shoulder, expecting a Chief Meade eager to appear involved in the town's latest crime. But instead she saw a rangy, lean figure with an unmistakable air of mystery . . .

No, wait, Vera thought, *that's just the fedora.* "Mr. Marvel!" she said. "Whatever brings you out here? Shouldn't you be signing books?"

"Sign books?" he asked. "And miss the real excitement? I heard the words *dead body* and knew I was needed. So!" He rubbed his paws together. "What have we got, Officer?"

"This is Deputy Braun," Vera explained. "We're lucky he was at the bookstore and could come to the crime scene so quickly."

"Sure, sure," Bradley said. "No one wants a crime scene to be tampered with. Say, it looks like a freshly dug grave here. The body looks to be wrapped in something, a bedsheet perhaps. Can't tell from here what species the poor bastard is."

As the wolf leaned over the open grave, Vera exchanged a glance with Orville, who just mouthed the words *Captain Obvious.*

Then Bradley pulled back sharply, waving a paw in front of his nose. "Whooo-whee, that's some stench. Wolves are highly sensitive to smell, you know."

"And what does your nose tell you about the victim?" Orville asked.

"Um . . . just that they're real dead. You'll have to exhume the body."

"That's usually the procedure," Orville replied. "But first . . ." He moved to the grave and leaned down over one end of the wrapped body. He tugged at the shroud covering the features of the victim. "I have to learn who or what this is."

With a deft tug, he flicked the cloth away from the body. Vera held up the lantern to give them a better view.

But she couldn't see any details of a face, and it took her a long moment to understand why . . . Then all the disturbing details coalesced.

"It's been beheaded!" Orville shouted, dropping the corner of the cloth in his surprise and mercifully hiding the gruesome truth. "Who could have done such a thing?"

Vera shook her head mutely, unable to answer. There was something very, very wrong here. Not just finding a body in the woods, but one so mutilated!

"Dr. Broadhead is going to have his work cut out for him," she whispered at last. And his work would be vital, because they'd need every tiny detail they could find to piece this crime together.

"This creature didn't die by accident!" Bradley declared.

Orville looked at the author and frowned but then apparently decided that shock had made the wolf momentarily idiotic.

"It's unlikely to be an accident," he conceded.

"Well, one thing is obvious," said the wolf after stating any number of very obvious things. "These woods are dangerous. And this sight has shocked poor Miss Vixen to the core."

"Vera?" asked Orville. "You all right?"

"Of course I'm all right," she said briskly. "I was just thinking about whether the beheading was the actual method of killing or if it was done afterward." Knowing that would help identify the murderer's possible mindset and motive.

"She's babbling," Bradley said. "Clearly too upset to function properly. You need to stay here, Officer, but I will escort Miss Vixen home to make sure she's safe. No fair creature should have to look on such a horrifying scene. Now, now, don't thank me," he added, though Orville had not been about to thank him. "Just doing my part."

Before Vera could say goodbye to Orville, Bradley was already steering her away from the crime scene and into the woods.

"Uh, town is in the other direction," she said as he tried to escort her along the path.

"Yes, of course!" he agreed, wheeling around the moment he understood he'd blundered the wrong way by 180 degrees. "Just wanted to get some distance between you and that hideous tableau. I'm surprised you didn't faint."

Fainting had never been Vera's style, but she acknowledged that the scene was not one she wanted to see again. "I hope Deputy Braun will be able to find out what happened and arrest the killer, if they can even be found."

"Wouldn't count on it. These Podunk cops don't know what to do when they see a real crime. When was the last time Shady Hollow experienced murder? Decades ago, I'll bet."

"Actually," Vera corrected, "just since I've moved here, there's been a poisoning, a drowning, a good old-fashioned blunt-object whacking . . . and that's not even counting the attempted murders."

Marvel's jaw dropped, and he took several seconds to think of a reply. "Er . . ." was his answer. "All committed by the same creature? Some madness overtook them?"

"Oh, no. Just the usual results of jealousy, greed, and thwarted love."

"Hey, I should really write a book set here. Can't use the

real name, of course. I'd have to tweak it to Spooky Hollow or Sleepy Hollow or . . . or *The Graves of Shady Grove*! That's got a ring to it."

"And would this be a Percy Bannon book?" Vera asked politely. By this time, they'd reached the more populated streets of downtown, and Vera nodded to a few residents walking home late and waved to a squirrel who was rearranging hats in the window of the millinery shop.

"No, no, no. Percy Bannon thwarts international criminals and crosses the globe. This would have to be a new character. A detective like no other . . . that gives me an idea." Marvel smiled at her.

For a moment, Vera experienced a vision of herself on a Marvel cover, dressed to the nines with her tail waving coquettishly. She began to say, "Oh, I'm not sure that I'd want—"

"A grizzled wolf down on his luck but always ready for the next case!" Bradley pulled his fedora low across his muzzle and flipped up the collar of his trench coat. "Wily. Astute. Keen-eyed. And strikingly handsome, of course."

"Of course." Vera sighed. Marvel was welcome to write his own personal fan fiction, but she hoped he wouldn't stay too long while he dreamed up his plot. "How long do you take to research your books, Mr. Marvel?"

"Call me Bradley," he told her, "and that's a great question. It depends. I rely on a few assistants for some of the work . . . the more routine queries and the boring stuff. Say, you're a reporter, aren't you? You know about fact-checking."

"Yes, it's a big part of the job." Even Gladys Honeysuckle made sure the gossip tidbits she chronicled weren't wildly off base . . . most of the time.

"You would be a good author assistant. In fact, I may venture to say you'd be a *marvelous* one." He grinned at Vera again, showing rows of sharp teeth. "How do you feel about that?"

"Um, thanks for the kind words," she replied, feeling that this stroll was interminable. Just then she spied the corner of her darling little house up the street. "Oh, look, we're here already! It was so nice of you to see me safely to my door, Mr. Marvel."

"A pleasure, and I told you to call me Bradley." He leaned toward her as though intending to kiss her.

Yikes. Vera stepped back, pulling her key from her bag as she did so. "You must be worn out from your talk at the bookstore, Mr. Marvel. I know I had a very full day. You ought to return to Bramblebriar to rest up. Good night!"

She unlocked her door and slipped through without opening it more than halfway. After turning the latch on the other side, she leaned against the door and sighed.

"What. A. Day." Vera eyed her quaint kitchen, where the teakettle waited on the stove. Yes, that's just what she needed. A nice cup of steamy chamomile tea, a few almond cookies left over from her last trip to the Bamboo Patch, and *no* wolves to interrupt her relaxation.

After the excitement of the bookstore event, compounded by the grisly discovery of a body in the woods, Vera was certain she would fall asleep immediately after brewing her tea, but instead, her brain churned through the events of the evening. She also pondered what Dot Springfield had said about Edward calling her by the wrong name at his mother's funeral.

Just as Vera settled onto her comfy couch, there was a knock at the door.

Vera groaned. If that wolf had come back to annoy her

again, Shady Hollow would have yet another murder to deal with.

"Vera? You still up? It's me."

"Orville!" she said happily, recognizing her beau's voice. She hurried to the door and opened it to let him in. "I'm so glad it's you."

"I thought I'd stop by to see that you're all right. I know it's not your first corpse, but it was still pretty grim."

"Definitely. Sit down," she said. After a brief search, she found the large mug Orville preferred to use when he was over. She poured chamomile tea into the mug and set it on the table next to the honey jar. "I don't think I could go to sleep without thinking some things through anyway."

"Me too," he agreed, stirring a healthy dollop of honey into his tea. "Without knowing the results of an autopsy, I'm one hundred percent confident that Ms. Brocket uncovered a murder. The way I figure it, some kids who were treasure hunting dug in that spot and partially exhumed the body. They got spooked and fled without covering the grave back up—"

Vera said, "Probably they're cowering in their families' homes right now, afraid of their own shadows."

He nodded. "But that meant a perfectly innocent creature, in this case Cassia Brocket, would walk through the woods and stumble over the now-open grave. Cassia knew right away that it was a police matter, so she reported it. But just think—if the treasure hunters had dug a few feet in any direction, that body might have stayed buried for years."

"You should find the kids," Vera said, "to confirm that's how it happened. I bet the rumors will be flying among the school set—you'll be able to figure out who happened upon the body without too much trouble."

"I'll do it tomorrow," he said with a nod. "And you?"

"What do you mean? I'll write up an article, of course. It's news."

"That's not what I mean, Vera. You're going to investigate because you think this is connected with the Springfield situation."

"I know it is," she said. "We don't know much about that body, but we've heard one recent accusation of murder, and now there's one corpse. That's not a coincidence."

"We don't know what it is yet," Orville said, a warning in his tone.

"Are you going to tell me I can't investigate? That it's too dangerous and you're going to use your power as the law to stop me?"

Orville put down his mug. "You'll keep sleuthing around no matter what I say. All I'm asking is that you be careful and keep me posted. We have no idea what's really going on here. But that corpse is missing a head, Vera. And anyone capable of killing, decapitating, and burying a creature is someone you need to be wary of."

That was very sensible advice, and Vera knew it. "You've got a point. And I don't intend to do anything stupid."

"At least not till after the election," he added with a hint of a smile.

"You're awful!" she said with a laugh. "And here I thought you liked me."

"Oh, I do," he said more seriously. "So you better take care of yourself."

"I promise," she said, touched by his concern. "And I promise to keep you in the loop."

"Good enough," he said, rising from his chair. "All right,

then. I've had a tough day, and tomorrow looks like it'll be even tougher. You lock your door tight, understand?"

"Sure, but which side of the door do you want to be on when I do?" she teased him.

He chuckled, gave her a kiss, and left to go to his own place. *He looks tired,* Vera thought as she watched him go. It wasn't fair to pile a murder on Orville's plate when he was also running for office.

Then again, when is murder ever fair?

After double-checking her door's lock, Vera went to her desk. She read over her notes about the Springfields and added some key points. It was starting to look like Dot might not be crazy after all. Perhaps Edward—the real Edward—had been murdered. Perhaps that was his body discovered in the woods. Perhaps Edward's long-lost brother, Thomas, had killed him and taken his place, certain that no one would notice the deception. He had not counted on Dot's natural instincts, nor did he have any idea what Edward called his wife in their intimate moments. He also hadn't expected the terms of his mother's will to be so complex.

Finally Vera decided that she had done as much as she could. She went to bed and tried to think about subjects more pleasant than murder and betrayal.

She thought about Orville and the upcoming election. It would be wonderful if he won the race for police chief. He worked so hard, and he really deserved it. Sometimes Vera allowed herself to daydream about a future with Orville. She was a career fox and did not often engage in romantic fancies, but every once in a while she wondered what it might be like to share her life and her home with another creature.

With this hopeful vision, Vera finally drifted off to sleep.

Chapter 12

After the excitement of the author event, the discovery of a body, and fending off the advances of a narcissistic wolf, it was perhaps not surprising that Vera overslept. She dragged herself out of bed, dressed quickly, and headed out to Joe's for a large cup of coffee.

Orville and Chief Meade were leaving the coffee shop just as Vera was entering. After a trio of good mornings, Orville mentioned that he and his boss were on their way to the hospital morgue to speak with Dr. Broadhead. Broadhead had worked all night and had the results of his preliminary report. Vera promised to join them just as soon as she concluded her business with Joe. She knew she would not survive this day without a great deal of coffee and perhaps an egg sandwich.

Fortunately the line at the counter was short, and Vera joined it while deeply breathing in the delightful aroma of coffee that filled the air. She spent her time waiting by studying the chalkboard menu written with the day's specials and was ready with her order when her turn came.

"Good morning, Joe," Vera greeted the moose. She kept the chitchat to a minimum since she knew he was busy. Joe Junior, the moose's son who usually helped out, was nowhere to be seen. "An egg-and-cheese sandwich on a sesame bagel with the largest coffee possible. To go, please."

"Coming up," Joe said cheerfully. He put in the order and motioned for Vera to wait on the bench near the door. The place was already filling up, and Lucy, a mink who'd been working as a waitress for quite a while, was directing newcomers to booths and tables like she was a tour guide.

A few minutes later, with her breakfast clutched in one paw and her coffee in the other, Vera was on her way to the morgue. She took her time so she could nibble at her bagel sandwich on the way. She wanted to appear professional when she arrived, not dripping with cheese and covered in coffee stains. Not to mention that food and forensics do not mix well.

When Vera entered the hospital, she went directly to the front desk, where a squirrel was entering some figures into a ledger. Vera identified herself and said she was there to meet with Dr. Broadhead. The squirrel stared at her for so long that Vera was afraid she had cheese on her face. Finally he directed her to the staircase.

"One flight down—exam room three."

Vera thanked him and made her way to the exam room, where she found Orville and Chief Meade awaiting the arrival of Dr. Broadhead.

Only a few minutes had passed when the police bears and the fox heard a very distinct slithering sound coming from the hallway. This heralded the return of the coroner, who greeted them all with great cordiality. The snake wasted no time in giving his preliminary report.

"The victim isss a male rat," Dr. Broadhead said. "I have determined that the decapitation happened possstmortem, but I have not yet determined the caussse of death. Alssso, identification isss sssomewhat complicated, asss the head is misssing. Therefore we cannot rely on dental recordsss. I would appreciate if the policssse could sssearch their own recordsss for reportsss of any misssing ratsss."

Vera and Orville were both scribbling down notes as the medical examiner made his report. Orville thanked Dr. Broadhead for his quick work and promised to let him know about the missing-creature reports. Chief Meade had given up all pretense of paying attention and was staring into space with a troubled expression. The deputy growled low in his throat to get the chief's attention. Meade started and then realized it was time to go.

Vera followed the police bears out of the morgue and up the stairs. At the front of the hospital, the group said their goodbyes. Orville and Meade were headed to the police station, and Vera wanted to have a consultation with Lenore. The raven would be cleaning up the bookshop after yesterday's large event. Vera decided to grab two more coffees from Joe's and then head over to Nevermore Books.

The bookshop was open for business but completely empty when Vera arrived. Lenore heard the bell over the door ring and made her way down from the office, where she'd been tallying up last night's receipts.

"Morning," Vera greeted her friend, offering her one of the coffees.

Lenore accepted the coffee with gratitude. "What perfect timing," the raven said, taking a sip. "I'm ready for a break. I gave Violet the day off so she could recover from all the excitement. What are you up to this morning?"

Vera also sipped her coffee and settled down to fill Lenore in on the events of the previous night and that morning. She realized Lenore had no idea that a body had been discovered in the woods. The raven had been too busy with customers at the signing to pay any attention to the deer's arrival or what had gone on afterward.

Vera relayed what had happened, leaving out the attentions of Bradley Marvel. She could tell her friend about *that* later. The important consideration now was that perhaps Dot Springfield was on to something after all. An unidentified dead rat was missing his head, and another murderer was likely running amok in Shady Hollow! Vera went on to share the highlights from the coroner's report.

Lenore sipped her coffee thoughtfully as she took it all in. Then she peppered Vera with questions. "Who would decapitate a rat, and why?" she began. "Was it an attempt to obscure the identity of the victim, or was there some other reason? Is the dead rat Edward Springfield? In that case, who is the rat posing as Edward Springfield?"

"Stop, stop," Vera begged her friend. "I don't know the answers to any of these questions. But I plan to find out. I have a theory about the Springfield family, although I'm going to have to travel to the town of Highbank to get more information."

"Highbank? Whatever for?"

"When I interviewed Edward, he mentioned his estranged brother, Thomas, had lived in Highbank for at least some time. And now, with the discovery of an unknown male rat, it seems like a good time to check out exactly what Thomas was doing in Highbank, if he ever left . . . and, if so, when!"

"You really think he could be involved? Thomas could just as likely be half a world away, living happily."

Vera said, "From both Edward's account and some reports I found in old newspaper clippings in the library, it's pretty clear that Thomas was a shifty individual. What if he returned to Mirror Lake because he heard Adora was close to death? Perhaps he wanted his share of the family fortune, and he intended to bully Edward into giving it over to him?"

Lenore's eyes gleamed with enthusiasm. "If there was blood in the foyer of the house, as Dorothy reported, then that means there was a fight. So, here are two theories: Thomas killed Edward and buried the body in the woods, then took over Edward's life in order to get the inheritance. *Or* Edward killed Thomas to keep Thomas from blackmailing him and buried the body, and Dorothy sensed something was wrong but came up with a typical Dotty-style conclusion."

"Of the two theories," Vera said slowly, "I think I'd go with the second. Thomas was older than Edward, and I can't imagine that the two look so much alike that it's fooling everyone in town. But *Edward* being the murderer and beheading Thomas to make sure no one ever identified the body as a Springfield makes a bit more sense."

"The only problem with that is . . ." Lenore began.

"Yeah. Everyone agrees that Edward is one of the nicest, most polite folks in town. He's not a murderer."

"Well," Lenore said, contradicting her previous suggestion, "anyone can become a murderer with the right motivation."

"I've got to go to Highbank and learn more about Thomas," Vera decided. "I'll head out tomorrow morning on the first boat upriver. Maybe Thomas is still there, alive and well and totally uninvolved in this mess. But maybe he's been missing for a couple weeks . . . exactly as long as that body's been in the ground."

Chapter 13

The next morning dawned clear and cool. It was perfect weather for both a boat ride and an investigative trip. The fox felt a rush of adrenaline as she dressed for the day. It was almost like having a day off but with the added excitement of possibly discovering some information about Thomas Springfield.

Stopping by the newspaper office, Vera poked her head into BW's private domain.

"Hey, Boss," she said, "just wanted to let you know that I'm chasing a story and I'll be out of the office for at least three days."

"What? That's an eternity in news!"

"Sorry, but I've got to go to Highbank, and I think I'll stay for at least two nights, possibly longer if I find something worth pursuing."

The skunk made a growling sound in his throat. "You'd better write the article of the year when you're done, Vixen. I'm not paying you to take vacations!"

"Sure thing, Boss," she said breezily as she left. Vera knew BW couldn't outrun her, so the conversation was effectively over.

Vera made her way to the dock with plenty of time to purchase a round-trip ticket to Highbank. The small town was upriver from both Shady Hollow and Mirror Lake; it would take most of the day to reach. Vera planned to spend two nights in Highbank, during which she would ask around town about Thomas Springfield, and then catch an evening boat back to Shady Hollow, unless she found a trail to follow. Geoffrey and Ben from Bramblebriar had a friend who ran a bed-and-breakfast in Highbank, which they recommended to Vera. She had also mentioned her plans to both Lenore and Orville so her absence wouldn't cause any undue worry. Plus it was easy (though not cheap) to send wingmail should she need to advise anyone of a change in plans.

Vera boarded the boat with a spring in her step. She knew from past trips that there was a small snack bar aboard that provided food and drink to passengers. Knowing there would be plenty of coffee available gave Vera peace of mind. She chose a seat on the upper deck and settled in for the journey. She had brought along a copy of *Watership Down*, and she was looking forward to a leisurely day of reading.

There were other passengers aboard the boat, but Vera kept to herself. She put down her book for a time and made some notes on what questions she wanted to ask about Thomas

Springfield. She planned to check into the inn and then find somewhere to have dinner. She would wait until the next day to ask around about the rat.

Vera considered herself to be an observant creature. Awareness was a big part of being an excellent journalist as well as detective. However, Vera was caught up in her musings, and she didn't think there was any reason for her to watch the other passengers. If she had looked around a little more carefully, she would have seen a particularly wolfish figure on the lower deck of the boat.

In the afternoon, when the boat neared the dock at Highbank, Vera reluctantly put down her book and gathered her belongings. She hated to stop reading at such a crucial point in the story! As she made her way down the gangplank to dry land, Vera asked one of the muskrat crew members for directions to Highbank Hideaway. The town was quite a bit smaller than Shady Hollow, so luckily everything she was looking for was conveniently located on the main street. The fox thanked the muskrat politely for his help and began climbing the many steps that connected the wharf to the town proper, which was situated on top of the bluffs. Once there, she made her way to the inn.

Highbank Hideaway was a charming Victorian set back from the street. It had a huge wraparound porch and an extensive garden with a gazebo. There were comfortable-looking wooden lounge chairs set in the garden. Vera hoped to claim one to read her book in after dinner. She went to the bright green front door and lifted the heavy knocker molded in the shape of a pineapple. The door was opened by an older lady chipmunk with a cheerful expression.

"Hello there, dear. My name is Kitty St. Clair. Welcome to Highbank Hideaway."

Vera was pleased to be greeted so cordially. She had not made a reservation but was hoping there would be a room available.

"I'm Vera Vixen," she replied. "I'm from Shady Hollow, and I am here on business. Might you have a room for a few nights?"

The affable chipmunk opened the front door wider and invited Vera into the vestibule.

"You are in luck, Miss Vixen," Kitty replied. "I have one of our finest rooms available. If you would like to sign our ledger, I can show you to your room."

Vera wondered if all innkeepers referred to every one of their rooms as "the finest." Kitty St. Clair was so similar to Ben and Geoffrey Eastwood that they could have been related. Perhaps it was just something they learned in the hospitality business.

Vera followed Kitty up the stairs and down a long hallway lined with closed mahogany doors. When they reached the end of the hall, they stood in front of a door with a shiny brass plate etched with a number 3. Kitty unlocked the door using a large key with a tag hanging from one end that declared: ROOM 3. The room boasted a large oak four-poster bed with a rose-colored coverlet and a score of fluffy pillows. Matching curtains hung over the windows. Two burgundy chairs even sat in front of a cozy-looking fireplace. Vera almost wished she could stay for a week. Perhaps she would!

Kitty St. Clair gave the key to her guest and turned to leave the room. "Enjoy your stay," the chipmunk said. "Breakfast will be available in the dining room tomorrow morning, and you can make tea or coffee anytime—it's all on the dining-room sideboard. If you need a recommendation for dinner, I'll be in the sitting room."

Vera breathed a deep sigh of contentment as the door to her room closed behind her hostess. It was such a luxury to have a beautiful room all to oneself and nothing pressing to do but decide what to have for dinner. Vera lay down on the bed, feeling rather like she was floating on a fluffy cloud. Her eyes slid closed and, without meaning to, she began to doze.

The chiming of the mantel clock woke her a half hour later. "Oh, dear!" Vera gasped. She hadn't meant to sleep on the job, and there was only so much time left in the day. There was fresh water in an ewer on the dresser, so Vera poured some into an accompanying bowl and washed her face and paws. Feeling refreshed, she went downstairs. She didn't encounter any other travelers, and she thought it was possible that she was the only guest.

Vera found Kitty in the sitting room knitting some type of garment in an extremely bright shade of green. Just as Vera was about to greet her hostess, her gaze went to the occupant of a wing chair near the fireplace. It couldn't be, but it was . . . a wolf in a fedora!

The chipmunk didn't seem to notice that Vera was frozen in the doorway with her mouth open. She greeted Vera pleasantly and said, "Have you met my other guest? This is Bradley Marvel."

Before Vera could respond, the wolf smoothly rose to his paws and gave her a toothy smile.

"Miss Vixen and I are old friends. Perhaps she would like

to have dinner with me at that charming bistro you recommended, Ms. St. Clair. What was it, the Blue Golf Club?"

Kitty giggled and corrected him. "The Blue Umbrella!"

Vera was flabbergasted by this turn of events and, unfortunately, still unable to regain her composure. She found herself walking down the front steps of Highbank Hideaway with the insufferable wolf while Kitty St. Clair waved from the front door like they were teenagers heading to prom.

Bradley Marvel did not seem to notice Vera's silence but yammered on about what a great book he planned to write inspired by Dotty Springfield and the Edward situation. Before Vera knew it, they had arrived at the restaurant: a pleasant-looking building with several outdoor tables, each with (as one might expect) a large blue umbrella.

A cheerful young rabbit offered a welcome and led them to a table for two in a corner of the large dining room. Bradley Marvel ordered a bottle of cider to share. At this moment, Vera finally recovered enough from her shock to speak.

"What on earth are you doing here in Highbank, Mr. Marvel?" She spoke quietly, but her anger was evident. "Did you follow me? What do you think you're doing? I'm here on serious business!"

"Calm down, Miss Vixen," the wolf replied, taking a large sip of his cider as he looked over the menu. "I know you're too shy to ask for my help, but I'm offering it to you."

Too shy? At this, Vera could actually feel her blood pressure rise. She took a sip of her own cider, which was crisp and delicious, and tried to compose herself.

She noticed that Bradley Marvel was looking at his menu with more and more concern. He beckoned their server over and demanded to know where a hungry wolf could get a steak in this town.

The server, who had told them his name was Nathaniel, began trembling as he nervously explained that the Blue Umbrella was, of course, a vegetarian restaurant. Marvel started to argue and then, realizing that Vera was staring at him with a most disapproving look, suddenly changed course and told Nathaniel he would have the mushroom risotto. Vera nodded and ordered the eggplant parmigiana. Nathaniel, who looked extremely relieved, wrote down their orders on a small notepad and brought them a basket of freshly baked bread.

Vera munched on the bread, sipped her cider, and glanced around the restaurant. She refused to make small talk with the wolf. When Nathaniel brought their entrées, she asked him if he had ever heard of Thomas Springfield.

The rabbit's eyes grew large. "Why, yes, miss," he replied. "The whole village of Highbank knows about Thomas Springfield. He ran up a tab in almost every store and restaurant in town, and then a few years ago, he vanished."

Vera's ears perked up. It seemed she was on to something.

"I was pretty young when it happened," the rabbit continued. "But folks say he owed money to some very sketchy creatures. I would check in with the local police if you want to know more. The police department is only a few blocks away."

Vera thanked Nathaniel for his information and turned her attention to the delicious-smelling plate in front of her. Bradley Marvel was already halfway through his bowl of risotto.

Nice manners, Vera thought, picking up her fork. Oh, well, she did not want him to think this was a date.

The party slurping risotto across the table notwithstanding, Vera was thoroughly enjoying her meal at the Blue Umbrella.

The service was friendly and attentive, and the food was outstanding. Not *quite* as good as the Bamboo Patch, but very close. She could almost pretend she was alone were it not for Bradley Marvel's ongoing stories of his own cleverness and bravery. She tuned him out as she planned her next move. It was still relatively early in the evening, and she was certain she could make a visit to the police station after dinner. She knew Orville often worked long hours staffing the station, and she assumed that Highbank's small-town police officers would be the same.

When Nathaniel came by with their bill, Vera thanked him for his information about Thomas Springfield and included a generous tip along with her half of the tab. She suspected that Bradley Marvel was the type of creature who didn't tip; he most likely assumed that the pleasure of waiting on him was compensation enough. Vera informed the wolf that she had paid her half of the check and that she was going to the restroom. She wasn't sure if he heard her, but she slipped from her seat and quickly exited the restaurant through a back door.

Vera felt almost giddy as she made her escape. The exit led to a back alley, and from there Vera found her way to the sidewalk. She looked around to see what other shops made up the business district of Highbank and spotted a theater almost directly across the street. According to the marquee, the current production was *The Taming of the Shrew*. The outside ticket window was empty, so Vera opened the door to the lobby. The play must have already started; she could hear dramatic voices from beyond the inner doors.

However, in the lobby, a bored-looking squirrel stood behind a beautifully constructed bar with wines and spirits lined up behind him. He straightened up when she entered.

"Welcome to the Highbank Theatre," he said, as if it was something he repeated many times a day. "The play has already started, miss."

"Hello," the fox replied. "My name is Vera Vixen, and I'm visiting from Shady Hollow. I don't need to see the play, but I'm hoping I can ask you some questions."

"Sure thing," the squirrel answered. His name tag said LANDON. "There's absolutely nothing going on here until intermission."

Vera thanked him and said, "I'm looking for some information about a Thomas Springfield, a rat by nature and by reputation. Ever heard of him?"

Landon had an expression on his face that told Vera he had plenty of news to share. She pulled out her notebook.

"Thomas Springfield was a nasty bit of goods," Landon began. "He was a deadbeat—owed money to almost every business and every creature in town. Had a habit of running up tabs and then neglecting to pay them."

Vera nodded, scribbling down notes as fast as he said them. She could tell that Landon enjoyed an audience (perhaps he was an aspiring actor). It was wonderful to interview a witness who was eager to talk, rather than have to drag information out of them. Not every creature was so willing to speak to the press.

Suddenly, Landon stopped his monologue. Vera looked up from her notebook.

"What is it?" she asked.

"I hate to be the one to tell you, Miss Vixen," he said dramatically, "but some folks are pure evil, and I'm afraid Thomas Springfield was one of them. Some of us wondered why he didn't live with his relatives in Mirror Lake. We came to find out they didn't want anything to do with him. But the facts might be too cruel for you to hear."

Vera was all too well acquainted with how malevolent individuals could be. She decided to keep that to herself and urged the squirrel to continue his story.

"Well, Miss Vixen, if you're sure," Landon went on. "The village of Highbank has a very active troop of Squirrel Scouts. My daughter Daisy is one of them. They do a lot of good in this town, and folks are always happy to contribute to their fundraisers by buying cookies. A few years ago, the scouts were raising money to go on a camping trip. My Daisy was so excited! She sold cookies day and night. Oddly enough, Thomas Springfield was one of her best customers. He bought two hundred boxes and claimed he would share them with his family when he visited Mirror Lake. Well, my Daisy and I delivered his cookies, but he never paid for them. I know we should have gotten the money up front, but I wanted my daughter to learn to trust folks. Instead, she learned that some folks are thieves."

Vera nodded sympathetically. "What happened then?" she asked.

"A few days later, that no-good rat disappeared. Needless to say, the Squirrel Scouts did not raise enough money to go on their camping trip. Daisy cried for a week. Most of us in town were of two minds—either he ran away to escape his debts or Big Eddie got him."

"Who's Big Eddie?" Vera asked.

"Um, I shouldn't have said that name. He's just . . . not someone to mess with." Landon looked upset, and Vera decided she wouldn't bother him with any more questions. She thanked him for his help and left the theater in search of the local law enforcement.

The Highbank police station was so tiny that it shared half its white-painted clapboard building with the post office. Vera walked in and found that the left side of the station featured neat rows of post office boxes on one wall and a counter, where a stoat in a jaunty pillbox hat stood smiling at her.

"Need to post a letter?" the stoat asked. "Or buy some stamps?"

"Actually, I need to talk to a police officer," Vera replied.

"Other side, dear," the stoat said, pointing to Vera's right, where a large walnut desk was positioned in one corner. A carved wooden chair was placed behind it, and two more were on the near side. "Just have a seat. She'll be with you shortly."

Vera sat down, wondering who wore the badge here in Highbank. She saw a nameplate on the desk that said OFFICER AMBLER, but there was no hint as to what creature the officer might be.

Just then, Vera sensed a presence behind her and turned to see a bobcat uniformed as a police officer regarding her with a sort of cool curiosity. The bobcat's approach had been dead silent. Vera suddenly had the sense that Highbank probably did not have too much difficulty with crime.

"I'm Philomena Ambler," the bobcat said, looking Vera up and down with a quick, intelligent glance. "What can I do for you, ma'am?" She sat in the chair behind the desk and picked up a pen, perhaps automatically, as if she was very used to writing reports.

"Good evening, Officer Ambler," Vera said. "I traveled from

Shady Hollow to learn anything I can about a creature who may have lived here, specifically a rat by the name of Thomas Springfield."

The bobcat looked much more alert now and gave Vera a second examination. Her tufted ears twitched just a tiny bit. "Looking for Springfield, eh. In what capacity?" she asked, still giving nothing away.

"I'm a reporter with the Shady Hollow *Herald*. Vera Vixen. Thomas's name came up in the course of a story I'm reporting."

Ambler relaxed. "That makes sense. Old Tom is how he was known around here, though he wasn't old when he lived here and he's definitely not getting any older."

"How's that?" Vera asked.

"Well, he's dead."

"What!"

"Oh, yes. A few years ago now. Just before I took this position, in fact. My predecessor had plenty of trouble with Old Tom, and I saw some of it, too, while I was helping out part-time."

"What happened? How do you know he's dead, Officer?"

"'Cause that's what his gravestone says. Thomas's body was found in the river one morning not too long after he tried to run away from Big Eddie, our local troublemaker. A bad-tempered otter who deals in stolen property, some smuggling, a little light moonshine production . . . and loans."

"Oh," Vera said, sensing what was coming. "Thomas borrowed money from Big Eddie and couldn't repay it?"

"Pretty much. Eddie will lend you fifty, but you'll be paying back one hundred fifty and you'll pay it when he says. Big Eddie is not to be trifled with. I'd arrest him if I could, but there are . . . complications." Ambler looked disgruntled as she said this, and Vera guessed that someone else in a criminal network was protecting Eddie.

"So you think this Big Eddie had Thomas killed?"

"I know it, though no one was officially charged with a crime. Eddie has a certain style, you see. Miss one payment, you lose a couple digits." The bobcat wiggled her paw meaningfully. "Miss the next payment, you lose more. Miss a third . . . well, there's a certain place in the river where we know to look. Eddie's eddy, we call it. We're very droll here in Highbank."

"You're sure the body was Thomas?"

"Eddie himself came down to identify the body. Said he recognized his old friend, which I took to mean that he recognized which toes he'd removed. A drowned rat is a very sad sight, especially one as skinny as Old Tom. He didn't eat well toward the end—he couldn't afford to."

"I'd like to see the grave," Vera said.

"Certainly. The cemetery is just up the road—"

The front door banged open, and a wolf walked in. "Oh, here it comes," Vera muttered under her breath.

"Vera, I thought I'd never find you!" Marvel announced loud enough for probably the entire town to hear. "What sort of backwater is this? I walked past four times before I saw that the police station is inside the post office!"

"We share the space," Ambler replied evenly.

Marvel turned, suddenly noticing that Highbank's cop was female. He leaned in, saying, "So you're the law in this town? Interesting! Very appealing for a twist on a thriller. I'm Bradley Marvel, by the way. You probably recognize me from the back of my book jackets."

"Huh," the cop said, not sounding too impressed. "I usually

recognize folks from their wanted posters. I'm Officer Philomena Ambler."

"Can I call you Philomena?"

"You can call me Officer Ambler," the bobcat said, just happening to stretch her forelimbs and extend her front claws a bit.

Bradley took a step back.

Vera glanced at her notes, asking, "Did Big Eddie offer any other clues about Thomas's activities?"

Ambler shook her head. "I was lucky he showed up to identify the body. Criminals like him don't often cross my path voluntarily."

"One more question, Officer," Vera said then. "Are you sure it's a gravestone and not a cenotaph?"

"What's a cenotaph?" Marvel asked.

"It's a memorial erected to commemorate the death of one who is buried elsewhere," Ambler said, then looked at Marvel with puzzlement. "Shouldn't you know words? I thought you were some kind of writer."

"I have assistants for that sort of thing," he said.

The bobcat rolled her eyes and looked back to Vera. "It's definitely a grave. I remember the funeral quite well, mostly because only my superior officer and I attended. We knew Old Tom best, you see. And even we weren't too cut up about his death."

"All right," Vera said. "I'm going to go have a look. Thank you, Officer Ambler."

"Call me Phil," the bobcat told her. "Head straight up the hill and take a left at the top. You'll see the cemetery from there. Old Tom was buried somewhere in the far corner. If you need anything else, you know where to find me."

Vera thanked her, jerked her head to indicate that Bradley should hustle, and started heading for the door.

Bradley pulled a couple bookmarks from his bag and laid them on Ambler's desk. "Just in case you're looking for an exciting new read," he said with a wink.

"I prefer the classics," she replied, not picking up the bookmarks.

"*Now*, Mr. Marvel," Vera said from the door. She strolled outside, half hoping he'd get lost but then thinking it wouldn't be very fair to either the cop or the postmistress to have to deal with him. Well, he'd catch up eventually.

Vera walked up the road to the top of the hill and turned left. She spotted the cemetery immediately. It was a ways out, just before the green wall of the forest. Advancing, Vera passed through an iron gate and in among the many plots. Highbank might not be a very big town, but it was established a long time ago, and the oldest stones were nearly unreadable, worn by erosion due to weather. Moss grew in the crevices of most headstones, and the graves set in deep shadow beneath large spreading trees were beset with ferns.

Using the last light of day, Vera walked methodically up and down the rows of gravestones, searching for more-recent burials. Remembering that Officer Ambler said she thought Thomas's grave was in the far corner, Vera went there, narrowing her search.

Several minutes later, she found it: a modest gray slab with Thomas Springfield's name and the formal phrase HE HATH LEFT THE WORLD OF THE LIVING, followed by a date three years prior. No sentimental rhymes, no BELOVED BY HIS FAMILY nor GONE BUT NOT FORGOTTEN. Thomas Springfield had left very

little mark on this world, and most of the folks who knew him
seemed as if they'd prefer *not* to have known him.

Vera gazed at the tombstone, frowning, and that was where
Bradley Marvel found her.

"What's going on?" he asked, slightly out of breath. "A lead?"

"The opposite of a lead," Vera grumbled. "A dead end.
Literally."

"How so?"

"I have two theories. One is that Thomas Springfield, the
ne'er-do-well son, somehow snuck back to Shady Hollow to
ingratiate himself with his brother, thinking that he could grab
his share of the inheritance. When that failed, he killed Edward
and began to impersonate him, using the family resemblance
to fool nearly everyone . . . until Dorothy returned. You can't
fool a wife! Alternatively, I imagine he came to the house and
there was a fight. Edward killed him in self-defense and then,
in a panic, buried the body in the woods to keep anyone from
asking awkward questions."

"Those could both work," Marvel said, scratching a few
notes in a notebook he'd produced from one of his trench coat
pockets.

"That's my point," Vera said. "They both *could* work . . .
until now. Thomas can't be the murderer or the victim of the
crime uncovered in Shady Hollow, because he is buried six feet
under here in Highbank and has been for the past three years!"

Chapter 14

Vera left the cemetery in decidedly ill humor. Part of that was due to one of her theories turning out to be totally wrong. Another part had to do with Bradley Marvel, who seemed glued to her side. The wolf kept spouting off about his books and the various ways in which his heroes solved crimes and defeated evil villains, all while remaining cool and suave enough to go out on the town afterward.

"You know," Vera said at last, as they were getting close to Highbank Hideaway, "I don't find all this discussion of other crimes very helpful when I'm thinking about *this* crime."

"Why do you care about this crime so much, anyway?" Marvel asked. "It's got nothing to do with you."

"The body was discovered in my town," Vera said. "I'm not going to sit back and let a murderer get away with that."

"Don't trust the cops, huh?" Bradley guessed. "Don't blame you. They both look like real bumpkins."

"Oh, really." Vera's tone was frosty now, but he didn't notice.

"Yep, that's always the way with these backwater burgs. The cops have just enough brains to put on the uniform but can't handle anything else."

"Is that what you thought of Officer Ambler?" Vera asked, opening the little garden gate that led to Highbank's bed-and-breakfast. She was impressed by the bobcat's intelligence and practical nature. Highbank was lucky to have her.

Marvel shrugged. "She seems sharper than most, but I can't say much for her taste in reading! Hey, how about we find out where the best drinks in town are?"

"Sorry, I'm going to have an early night," Vera said. In truth, she couldn't wait to get away from the persistent wolf. "Maybe I'll see you tomorrow."

She went inside before he could reply. Vera took the stairs up to her room and opened the door to find that Kitty had already done the turndown service. Vera's bed linens were neatly folded and the numerous decorative pillows had been moved to a side bench, so she could slip into bed whenever she was ready. On the nightstand, a tray held a small carafe of fresh water and a tiny plate with a few homemade mint candies.

"Oh, thank you!" Vera murmured. She didn't always want to be pampered, but sometimes it sure helped.

She shrugged out of her traveling coat and hung it up, still musing about what she'd learned today and whether this trip to Highbank was worth anything in terms of solving the murder.

"I'm no further than I was a week ago," she said out loud in disgust. "All I've done is find a blind alley."

Granted, it was good to know that the line of inquiry into Edward's brother could end right here. She'd been so sure that she'd done some clever detective work! But the identity of the victim was still unknown . . . and Dorothy's accusation was still unanswered.

"Ugh," Vera muttered. She popped one of the mints into her mouth and found it deliciously cool. "I should just stop sleuthing for the night. A new idea will come to me in the morning."

She changed into her favorite silk pajamas and found her book in her luggage. Tucking herself into bed, she tried to focus on the tale instead of the knotty problem she was trying to solve. She fell asleep reading, which is a fine way to fall asleep. Indeed, Vera slept so soundly that she didn't even twitch when something was slid under her door in the darkest hour of the night.

Vera awoke the next morning in her lovely room. After she washed her face and paws and got dressed for the day, she finally noticed a small envelope resting on the rug in front of the doorway. She snatched it up and ripped the flap open. There was a folded sheet of paper inside that read: *The rat lived in a cabin on Acorn Way.*

The note said nothing else, nor was it signed. Vera thought perhaps it was from Officer Ambler. But in any case, the timing was perfect—she would investigate this clue immediately after breakfast! She had the whole day free to ask questions about Thomas Springfield.

The fox made her way downstairs to the dining room,

where breakfast was available. Vera was relieved to see that Bradley Marvel wasn't up yet. With any luck, she could have a quick meal and ask her hostess where Acorn Way was before she encountered the wolf.

The mahogany sideboard in the dining room was set with everything a creature could want for breakfast. There were bowls of sliced fruit and yogurt and a large tureen containing oatmeal with brown sugar. There was also a chafing dish filled with fluffy scrambled eggs. Best of all, there was a platter of delicious-looking freshly baked crumb cake.

"This is the life," Vera said as she filled her plate. She also poured herself a mug of coffee from a carafe. Wouldn't it be nice to have breakfast like this every day?

When Kitty St. Clair popped into the room to remove the dirty dishes, Vera took the opportunity to ask the chipmunk for directions to Acorn Way. It was some distance from the center of Highbank, but Vera was feeling quite full, and a walk would do her good.

After she thanked Kitty for such a lovely meal, she went back up to her room for a hat. She could hear loud snores echoing from a closed door down the hall. Vera was happy that she could continue her sleuthing without the wolf's unwelcome assistance.

The fox trotted briskly up the road, following the directions that Kitty St. Clair had given her. It was a beautiful crisp day, and Vera's spirits rose as she mulled over the information she knew about Thomas Springfield. Her theories were ruined now that she had discovered Thomas had been dead for three years. She would have to come up with a new concept to fit the facts. Furthermore, there had been no exact identification of the headless corpse found in Shady Hollow, so it was possible the answer would be entirely different once they learned who'd been killed.

After some time, Vera turned onto a dirt road with a home-made sign that informed her she was on Acorn Way. She was well away from Highbank now, and it had been ten minutes since she'd seen a house. The surroundings were peaceful, though. It was so nice to be able to formulate her thoughts without Bradley Marvel rambling in her ear. She'd thought she might have trouble figuring out which cabin had belonged to Thomas Springfield, but there seemed to be only one residence on this deserted dirt road. She approached the dilapidated dwelling cautiously.

There was a rotten mailbox attached to the siding next to the front door. It had a label that was partly gone, with only the letters SPRINGF left to read. The door was closed but not locked. Vera knocked just in case, but after a long silence, she pushed it open. She stood on the threshold for a moment but heard no movement from within. This cabin must have been sitting empty since the rat's death three years ago.

The cabin was basically one room, with a bare cot on one side and a tiny kitchen on the other. The furniture, such as it was, had been left behind, but there were no personal items in sight. No clothes nor toiletries anywhere.

A slight sound, like the creaking of a floorboard, made Vera spin around and face the wall behind her, but there was nothing unusual to be seen—just a bare curtainless window looking out onto the overgrown front yard.

Pushing away a slight feeling of creepiness, Vera continued her search. But there was almost nothing to be found here. No pictures or books on the small sad-looking shelf above the table and its lone dining chair. Vera checked the cabinets in the kitchen and the small dresser that stood next to the cot. All were empty.

"So much for finding a clue," she muttered. This excursion to Thomas's cabin had been a waste of time.

As Vera exited the ramshackle building, she thought about the best way to get back to town. Following Kitty St. Clair's careful directions—which were designed to prevent one's getting lost and not for maximum efficiency—Vera had taken the long way, traveling along a road from the village. While there was undoubtedly a more direct route through the woods that locals would know about, Vera decided it would be foolish for her to try to navigate her way through the unfamiliar territory.

Just then, Vera caught sight of something within the deep shadows of a grove of pine trees to the west. A creature-sized mass pulling just out of her view.

Vera remembered the creepy feeling of being watched. Had some animal been peeking at her through the window? She quickened her pace, trotting away from the cabin and into the woods toward where she'd seen that hint of movement.

As she neared the pine grove, a shadow detached from the general gloom and shuffled away along a narrow path scarcely wide enough for a single creature to follow.

"Hey!" Vera yelled. "Who's there? You can talk to me! It's safe. I'm just a reporter. Won't you come here?"

But the shadow did exactly the opposite, now running at a faster pace. Vera noticed a glint of silver on the ground and saw that the creature had dropped something—maybe a coin or two?

She had no time to pick it up and examine it further. Vera squinted as she increased her pace to catch her quarry. Was the creature a weasel? Or a rat? A stoat, perhaps? The shifting patches of light from the tree canopy provided natural camouflage, and it was impossible to tell.

"Hey, I'm not going to hurt you!" Vera called. "I just want to ask a few questions!" She didn't really expect the second invitation to go any better than the first, and indeed, the creature now began to weave along the path, using the overgrown shrubs to create momentary shields that blocked Vera's sightlines as she chased them down the narrow winding track. As Vera jogged along, she kept her gaze pinned to the elusive creature ahead of her, worried that if she lost sight of them for even an instant, she'd miss them here in the deep forest.

All of a sudden Vera realized the firm dirt path beneath her had become soft. No, not soft—gone completely! She desperately paddled thin air for an interminable moment and then fell down, down, down.

Vera hit hard ground without warning and groaned at the pain of impact. She took a few deep breaths and then slowly opened her eyes.

She was at the bottom of a very deep hole in the middle of the woods. The sides were perfectly vertical and very smooth, the consistency that of wet clay. Vera stood up and took a step, and her paw nudged a large springy pine bough that had fallen into the hole along with her. A few more were scattered about.

She'd literally run into a trap. The pine boughs had covered the opening of the hole in the middle of the narrow path. If she'd been walking at a normal pace, she likely would have spotted the trick and moved off the path to make her way through the brambles instead. The mysterious creature had moved quickly, though not so fast that Vera would lose track of them and give up the chase.

"I'm an idiot," she said out loud. The close, soft walls of the pit absorbed the sound of her voice, making her feel even more alone.

It now seemed clear that Vera had been lured out to the woods by the anonymous note left under her door at the inn. Surely if Officer Ambler had sent the note, she'd have signed it and probably offered to come with Vera. Vera knew what cops were like!

"Oh, Orville's going to be so mad," she said. Hadn't he warned her about exactly this sort of thing? Running after a lead without talking to anyone else first?

Well, she had done so anyway, and now here she was, in a hole in the middle of nowhere, and no creature knew where except the one who put her there. *Oh, no,* she thought, looking up at the circle of sky above her. What if they came back to finish her off?

"Help!" she shouted as loudly as she could. "Help! Is anyone there?"

She tried to climb the walls, but her paws sank into the muddy surface and sent her sliding right back down to the bottom, ruining any progress she might have made.

"Help!" she howled again, knowing that no one was likely to hear her.

Vera tried to calm herself and think rationally. She was a small fox at the bottom of a very deep hole, and there was no way to climb out. She couldn't count on Orville or Lenore realizing that anything was wrong, as she was not expected home until the end of the next day! Then Vera brightened. Kitty St. Clair knew Vera was planning on visiting Thomas Springfield's abandoned cabin, because Vera had asked for directions. But her spirits sank once more. Kitty would not miss Vera until at least dinnertime, and perhaps not even then, since she'd assume her guest was simply out and about town.

Panic rose in Vera's chest. There had to be a way out of this mess. She took several deep breaths and tried to compose herself. She had been in dangerous situations before. She could figure this out.

She picked up one of the pine boughs. Could she break it into pieces and jam the wooden stakes into the walls, creating a series of pawholds to the surface? She gnawed at one end of the bough, as she had no other method of cutting. Ugh! Sticky sap and the worst sort of ginny taste! Grimacing, she kept at it.

Then she paused. Vera thought she heard a creature calling her name very faintly.

"Vera?" a voice demanded. "You out here? Hellooooo?"

"Yes!" Vera answered, her voice quavering at first, then growing as she put her heart into it. "Yes! Who's up there? I'm down here in a pit. Watch your step!" The last thing she needed was another body down here with her.

"Vera!" the voice said, much closer. "What are you doing down there?"

She looked up to where the voice was coming from and spotted the brim of a fedora.

"Oh, for pity's sake," she muttered to herself. It was none other than the persistent Bradley Marvel. He must have asked Kitty where Vera went and then followed the same directions.

Well, any port in a storm . . .

"I need to get out of here!" she yelled. "Find a rope or fetch Officer Ambler, or something. Hurry!" Vera had not forgotten the creature who led her into this trap; it was still quite possible that it would return.

"Oh, I know what to do," Bradley said, shrugging out of his

trench coat. "A scene just like this occurred in *High Stakes*, the third Percy Bannon book. He goes to the jungle nation of the tiger queen . . . Very gripping. You must remember it?"

"Sorry, I'm a little distracted right now," Vera replied through clenched jaws. (This irritation was not fully a result of the author's assuming she was familiar with his entire oeuvre; she also had some pine sap stuck in her teeth.)

"Understandable," he said kindly. "Anyway, it goes like this: The tiger princess falls into the pit—it's actually called a tiger trap, did you know?—and Percy finds her. He ties his scarf and shirt together, then lies down and lowers the makeshift rope into the pit. *Great* image, don't you think? My publisher wanted it on the cover, but I said it would be a spoiler. Anyway . . ." Bradley demonstrated the story as he spoke, and soon the wolf's long coat dangled tantalizingly close.

"Okay, hold tight," Vera said. "I'm going to jump up and grab the sleeve!" She crouched, sprang directly up, and snatched the hanging sleeve of the coat in her paw. "Pull!" she shouted.

With a grunt and a series of muttered curses, Bradley pulled the coat up by inches. Vera heard a seam rip and prayed the coat was well-made enough to last through the rescue.

"Almost . . . there . . ." Bradley gasped out.

Vera pawed at the wall to help her progress along, and just as the coat stretched to its breaking point, she reached the rim of the pit and grabbed for it with both paws. She scrambled to the surface, panting when she cleared the pit and could lie on the path to catch her breath.

"Hmm, this coat's done for," Bradley said, examining the wreckage.

"I'll pay for another," said Vera. *The oaf did save my life with it, after all.*

Marvel put the coat back on, examining the effect. "I suppose I can think of it as a disguise. So why were you in that pit? Following a clue?" He held up the silver coin Vera had seen earlier. "This was lying on the path; it's why I walked as far as I did."

"Yes," Vera said. "A creature was spying on me while I was looking over Thomas's old cabin. I followed them, and they dropped a couple coins . . . but clearly it was all a setup in order to get me out of the way."

Bradley looked stunned and delighted. "That means I saved you! Life imitates art!"

Vera suppressed a sigh. "Unfortunately I couldn't identify the creature at all, so I don't know who to look for now. And I can't tell the police anything about who it might be."

She started back down the path, hoping to get back to town as soon as possible. Bradley Marvel was close on her heels.

"You know, this whole thing might be a bit out of your league, Vera. Didn't that cop mention a criminal called Big Eddie? You could be in over your head!"

Considering she'd been in *well* over her head while stuck in that pit, Vera couldn't dispute Bradley's words. But she also didn't like it when folks tried to kill her.

"I'm going to solve this case," she muttered. "If it's important enough to shut me up, it's important enough to uncover the truth."

"How are you going to solve the case now that your main suspect's turned out to be long dead?"

"First thing," Vera said, feeling gross and dirty and very angry, "is to take a bath."

Chapter 15

Thankfully, the rest of Vera's stay in Highbank was uneventful. She stopped by the police station only to learn that Philomena had not sent any note.

"Ugh. I'm an idiot, running after a false trail," Vera said, disgusted with herself.

"I'll go out there later and look around," the bobcat told her. "Maybe I can pick up a clue or identify some prints. My bet is that Big Eddie is involved somehow. If I discover anything, I'll message you in Shady Hollow. In the meantime, I suggest you stay here in town and keep your investigations to chats with the locals. You might find some more information if you go to Elmo's Bar for dinner tonight. The place looks like a dive, but the food is amazing. Everything that can be fried will be fried. You'll meet plenty of folks there who will talk."

Vera thanked Philomena and continued on to Highbank Hideaway. Kitty St. Clair was extremely solicitous when she saw the state of Vera's clothes and fur. "My, what happened to you?" she cried.

"A rather steep fall," Vera explained, "and it hurt a lot when I hit the bottom."

Without a further word, Kitty arranged a deep soak for Vera in a large copper tub full of steamy water and a cloud of bubbles. "You poor thing," Kitty fussed. "Enjoy the bath just as long as you like, dear. Here are the towels, and I'll bring a tray of tea up to your room so you can refuel when you're done. We don't want you catching your death of cold due to wet fur!"

Vera soaked in the hot water, feeling physically better but mentally drained from the thoughts cycling in her head. Who had tried to hurt her? Had that trap been dug just for her, or was it there before? If Thomas was dead, why would Big Eddie or his minions care whether Vera poked her nose into the case? And, if Thomas was dead, *then who was the rat buried in the woods by Shady Hollow?*

Nothing made any sense, so Vera gave up for the moment. She stayed in the tub till the water cooled. After her bath, she applied herself to drinking the wonderfully spicy tea that had been brought to her room along with a plate of hearty scones, which she slathered in clotted cream and fig jam.

Either the tea or the scones had healing qualities, because Vera was soon ready to pursue more information about Thomas or Big Eddie or whatever clues she could sniff out. She went in search of Elmo's Bar, which was located on the riverfront. Since Highbank featured bluffs along the shore, Vera had to climb down a few long flights of rickety stairs bolted into a cliff face. She wondered how guests who drank too much managed to climb back up. At the bottom of the stairs, she saw a short pier hosting several rowboats, which were lashed to posts. Each boat held drowsing figures.

"Ah," she said to herself. "So they don't climb back up till they sleep it off."

Elmo's Bar was a clapboard structure perched on the narrow bank. Unlit lanterns hung from the eaves, and fishing nets festooned the outer walls. A sign with blue letters proclaimed:

ELMO'S BAR

YOU CAN'T GO LOWER THAN HERE

Vera pushed the door open. Inside, the place was dimly lit and, despite the time being well before sundown, half the seats were occupied. The patrons looked to be mostly sailors and stevedores alongside several folks whose occupations were unclear (or possibly nonexistent). Eyes raised to survey Vera as she entered. Some tones shifted from conversational to curious, but no one said anything to her. She walked up to the bar and snagged an empty seat.

A muskrat serving behind the counter swiped a rag across the wooden bar top and asked, "What'll it be, duchess?"

"Have you got any Cold Clay Spiked Cider?"

The muskrat nodded in cautious approval. "Coming right up."

Vera watched as the muskrat drew a glass of hard cider from a tap. He placed the tumbler in front of Vera. She took a long drink and smiled. "Perfect. I wondered why you want your customers to walk all those steps outside, but now I figure it's because they get so thirsty on the way down."

The bartender chuckled. "Got it in one." He reached under the bar and pulled out a small shallow basket filled with salty peanuts. "Here you go. Just in case the stairs didn't get you thirsty enough. Fan of cider, are you?"

"I like Cold Clay Orchards'. I'm from Shady Hollow," she added.

"Supporting your local brew, then." He nodded. "Excellent. I'm Elmo, by the way. Just holler if you need a refill."

The muskrat moved farther down the bar to serve drinks to another customer. Vera sipped her drink and nibbled on the bar nuts, which were not just salty but also seasoned with an herby mix of flavors: chives, thyme, pepper, and a hint of rosemary. It was surprisingly addictive, and Vera could imagine ordering more drinks to complement the taste.

A creature slid into the seat next to her. She looked over to see a black rat holding a half-full beer and examining her with an intelligent, watchful gaze.

"Bit early for a refill," Vera noted easily.

"Give me a minute and it won't be," the rat responded just as easily. "But I'm more interested in meeting a new face. Haven't seen you around town."

"I'm visiting," Vera said. "My name's Vera, and I'm a reporter with the Shady Hollow *Herald*. I'm here for a story. And what's your name?"

"Wiley." The rat looked intrigued. "Story, huh. What about?"

"I'm looking for information about a rat named Thomas Springfield."

"You're a little late, then. He took a dive a few years ago."

"So I heard. Did you know him?"

The rat wrinkled his nose. "Sad to say I did. He was a steady fixture here, actually. He didn't work the water, not on a boat or on the shore, but he sure did like the atmosphere. Talked up a storm about this and that and how he was the smartest rat in the room. Huh. If he was so smart, how'd he get so dead?"

"Tragic accident?" Vera suggested.

Wiley laughed. "If you want to call falling off the bluffs with your limbs bound an accident, then sure."

"I hear he knew Big Eddie," Vera added more quietly.

"Best not to bring up that name," the rat cautioned. "That's attention you don't want. You'd never live long enough to write any story for your *Herald*. Hell, you wouldn't make it back to the ferry."

"He's that dangerous?"

Wiley glanced over Vera's shoulder. "Don't turn your head now, but if you did, you'd see a half dozen of Big Eddie's gang. They've been watching you since you walked in. And not just because they like your looks." He grinned then. "Though there's nothing wrong with your looks."

"Why, thank you," Vera said with a laugh. "Tell me, did Thomas Springfield chat with those folks when he hung out here?"

"Often enough, until the end. He avoided this place for the last few weeks of his life, since they wanted to *chat* with him, if you take my meaning. But in happier days, sure. He'd nurse a drink all night and cram a whole pound of those bar snacks in his piehole. Poor Elmo—the snacks are free, but everyone knows it's rude to take more than their share."

"But Thomas didn't know that?"

"Old Tom didn't *care*," Wiley said, spitting on the floor. "That rat deserved what he got. Vicious through and through."

Vera finished her drink, and Wiley offered to walk her back up to the main street. "Not that Eddie's gang would do anything, but don't give 'em ideas, huh?"

Thinking of the mysterious figure who landed her in a pit earlier, Vera agreed that an early exit would be best. She paid her tab to Elmo and allowed Wiley to escort her all the way back to Highbank Hideaway.

Wiley whistled. "Huh. Nice digs, I hear. And Kitty sure can cook. Maybe I should have been a reporter instead of a stevedore!"

With a smile, Vera thanked him for the information and the walk. "I'm leaving for Shady Hollow tomorrow. Looks like my trip here didn't tell me what I wanted to know."

"Some things are better left buried," Wiley said, with no idea of how close his phrase hit. "You have a safe journey home, Miss Vera."

"Good night, Wiley," Vera said, waving as she stepped inside the bed-and-breakfast. The trip hadn't been totally in vain, but she still had more questions than answers. Alas, it seemed that poking around in Big Eddie's business might be bad for her health. A few years ago Vera would have plunged right in, heedless of the consequences. But she was a little older and wiser now, she hoped. And she had a firm cap of one life-threatening situation a week. The last thing she wanted was to get tossed over a bluff by Big Eddie or his goons.

Her room had been turned down for the night once more, and she looked at the big fluffy bed with delight. A few moments later, she was snuggled down under the comforter.

"I'll just close my eyes for a second," she said. "Then I'll go over my notes."

She closed her eyes . . . and went right to sleep.

When Vera opened her eyes the next morning, she wondered for a moment why all her limbs ached. Then she remembered the events of yesterday and groaned a little as she climbed out of bed. She would have one more luxurious breakfast at High-bank Hideaway before the midmorning ferry for Shady Hol-low. She was ready to be in her own house and to see Lenore and Orville.

Once more the dining room was set up with an ample repast. Today there were pancakes and fruit. Vera filled her plate with the delicious food and filled a mug with coffee. She was congratulating herself on dodging Bradley Marvel when the wolf entered the dining room. Vera knew there would be no avoiding him on the boat home, so she resigned herself to be as cordial as she could. After all, if not for Bradley Marvel, she would still be trapped at the bottom of a pit . . . or worse.

"Good morning, Vera," the wolf boomed, clearly in good humor. "You don't look any the worse for wear after your fall."

"I'm feeling much better," Vera replied, and then, because she knew he'd be expecting it, added, "Thanks to you, I'm alive to tell the tale."

Bradley Marvel nodded modestly, but he was obviously pleased. He'd fancied himself a hero, and now he actually was one. Vera shuddered to think what could have happened if he had not found her.

Vera finished her pancakes as quickly as she could. She excused herself, saying she needed to pack up her things and get to the dock. The wolf nodded and said he would see her on the boat.

The ride back was tolerable, and when the boat docked at Shady Hollow, Vera knew the first order of business was a proper dinner. She'd made the mistake of mentioning that she loved the food at the Bamboo Patch, and before she knew what was happening, Bradley Marvel was walking her to the restaurant and, once there, loudly announcing that they needed a table for two. Several other diners glanced their way, inquisitive looks on their faces.

Oh, brother, Vera thought. She wasn't sure she could endure another meal with Marvel. *Maybe I can tell Sun Li I need takeout.*

They were seated at a comfortable booth near the kitchen, and Vera concentrated on the divine smells coming from there rather than on her dinner companion.

"Pearl Mountain–style Mushroom Steak, huh?" Bradley said, perusing the menu. "Now that's more like it!"

"I'll have the Three-Treasure Squash," Vera told the server, "and some tea, please."

"Of course, Miss Vixen," the server said with a smile. "Chrysanthemum, as usual?" At Vera's nod, she hurried away to get the teacups.

Vera sighed. At least her tummy would be satisfied. Her brain was not so lucky.

"I just don't know how to explain what happened in the woods," she said, scanning her notebook, hoping for a spark of inspiration.

"It's simple," Bradley said.

"Really?"

"You were in dire peril, and I saved you—"

"Not those woods," she interrupted crossly. "I mean the woods here in Shady Hollow, where the body was discovered. If that corpse isn't Edward, and it isn't Thomas, then who could it be? No other male rats were reported missing in this area; Orville checked the records. We don't attract many folks just passing through, especially not this late in the year. They come because they've got family here or they're looking for work."

The server returned to the table with a tea tray. She set the ceramic teapot down and then placed a teacup in front of each of them. The cups were decorated with beautifully painted maple leaves in red and yellow. Sun Li liked to have dishes that matched the season—it was all part of the charm of dining here.

Bradley took a sip and scalded his tongue.

"Careful, it's hot," Vera warned him halfheartedly. Then she continued, "I refuse to believe a stranger just happened to wander into town and then just happened to get killed by someone who just happened to bury them without being seen! It's ridiculous."

"If no one cares that the rat is dead, why bother finding out what happened?" Bradley asked.

Vera carefully sipped her tea from the half-filled cup; it was now the perfect temperature. "*I* care that the rat is dead. And, anyway, it's still important to find out the truth."

She thought of Mr. Fallow's request for her to investigate the crime. If Vera couldn't prove that the corpse was some-how connected to Dorothy's accusation that Edward was somehow not really Edward, then it was quite possible that Dorothy would be declared mentally ill. Vera couldn't stand to see Dorothy shut away for the rest of her life simply because the rat couldn't prove what she felt in her heart to be true. "I've got to find some evidence that will help Dot," Vera said at last.

Just then, Sun Li himself came out bearing a tray with two large plates. "Heard you were here, Vera," he said, putting a plate down in front of her. "How goes the investigation?"

"Not great," she admitted. "Every time I think I have a lead, it ends up being a red herring."

"Huh, good thing you didn't order the special, then," Sun Li joked. He looked at Bradley Marvel. "Is this a friend?" (Sun Li was one of the few creatures who hadn't appeared at the book signing.)

"Bradley Marvel. Author. Adventurer. Alpha. Oh, and I saved Vera's life yesterday," Bradley told the chef.

"Well, that is certainly a good deed," Sun Li replied politely. "Enjoy your dinner. And, Vera," he added, "if you keep risking your life while solving murders, you know you're going to make a lot of folks upset."

"Yes, sir," she said with a little salute.

Vera focused on her meal and enjoyed it immensely. A fall favorite, it consisted of three kinds of grilled squash arranged over a pilaf of three kinds of rice. Drizzled over it all was a sweet sauce with ginger, cinnamon, and pepper—the aforementioned three treasures.

Meanwhile, Bradley poked at his steak. "I think this whole thing is *made* of mushrooms," he decided sadly. Apparently he had not realized that this restaurant was also entirely vegetarian. "I can't wait to get back to the city."

What's keeping you? Vera wanted to ask. After all, his tour event was done, and he showed remarkably little interest in solving the case. He only followed Vera around . . . maybe for research on his next book?

Vera sadly skipped dessert, mostly to get home sooner. Sun Li slipped her a few almond cookies wrapped in a bright red rice-paper envelope and wished her good luck with the investigation.

As they walked through the serene patch of bamboo that hid the restaurant from the main street, Bradley asked where they were going next, taking for granted that they were going together.

"I want to stop by the police station to see if Orville—I mean Deputy Braun—is working. If he's not there, I'll go to the campaign office. I need to talk to him about what I found in Highbank."

"So you're a reporter, a private detective, and a cop? Sounds like you're doing everyone's job for them. You don't need to rush off to find that dumb bear." Unexpectedly, Bradley leaned in close and said, "Come away with me, to the city! There's so much more there." He looked like he was about to kiss her.

Vera ducked and stepped out of kissing range. "Are you dense? Orville and I are dating. I'm not spending time with him to solve a crime; I'm spending time with him because I *like* him."

"That rotting stump? You can't possibly be attracted to him. My word, Vera, I just offered you a ticket out of this backwater. You can live in the big city, go to parties, have fun. You'll love being my assistant!"

"About as much as I'd love being covered in wasps," she retorted. "If you listened to anyone besides yourself, you'd remember that I'm *from* the city. I came here for a change. And the day I give up my career to type press releases is the day you'll know I've been replaced by an impostor! Now go back to Bramblebriar, pack your bags, and walk to the dock, because if you're not on the next boat downriver, I'll tell Orville to arrest you for being an idiot in public, which is against the law in Shady Hollow!"

"It is not," Bradley countered as though by instinct.

"Town Ordinance 142, drafted by the first sitting council after the town's founding," she recited. "Now get moving!"

Vera's lips had curled back in a snarl, and she'd bared her very sharp teeth. Despite being larger, and likely tougher, Bradley Marvel slunk backward, cowed by her fury.

"All right, all right," he muttered, his yellow eyes darting left and right as if checking to see whether they'd been overheard by anyone. But they were still alone. He began talking under his breath: "Didn't want to stay, anyway. Got places to be . . . This dump is boring. Can't believe my publicist wants me to work on a small-town thriller story . . . So stupid . . . Nothing ever happens here . . . Yeah, that's what I'll tell him. Got to go where the action is . . ." He walked off, still revising his story to better suit his vanity.

Vera let Bradley go, too tired to bother correcting his version of events. *Nothing ever happens here? Ha!* Marvel didn't have the chops to deal with small-town life . . . or death.

Chapter 16

Vera watched the wolf stalk off to the bed-and-breakfast, presumably to fume until he could scamper onto the next boat heading for the city. Then she went directly to the police station, hoping to find Orville and to talk over what she'd learned in Highbank. However, only Chief Meade was there, so Vera merely asked where the deputy was.

"His campaign headquarters, probably," Meade responded. "He seems to live there when he's not working."

"You still hoping to have a debate with him before the election?" she asked politely.

"Huh, after a fresh body was discovered and the crime remains unsolved? No chance! I don't want the whole town to show up with pitchforks."

"I'm sure you'll solve it soon," Vera said. "Any more clues so far?"

He shook his head. "Hardly anything, except that Broadhead found a knife wound in the victim's chest. So we know how the poor bugger died, but not who he was."

After saying good night to the chief, Vera proceeded to Orville's campaign headquarters. She didn't particularly care for the building that housed it (she had some bad memories of her time there), but she knocked anyway. In a small office on the first floor, a ferret greeted her.

"Evening, Miss Vixen. If you're looking for Deputy Braun, he left for the Riverside Pub an hour ago. We set up a little event where folks can ask him questions in a casual setting. Good, huh?"

"Brilliant," Vera agreed.

"I'm just locking up the office now, but if you hurry, you can make the last part of the event."

"I'll just find him tomorrow, thanks." Vera wanted to talk with Orville, but she hated the thought of interrupting his campaigning to do so. The news she'd discovered would keep overnight. Besides, she'd just realized how tired she was. Although foxes do not hibernate, the old tradition made perfect sense—Vera wanted to sleep until spring!

At her house, she dropped her bag inside the door and crawled into bed. It might not have been as fancy as the beds at Highbank Hideaway, but there is a special joy in returning to one's own cozy, rumpled nest.

Vera fell asleep instantly.

A pounding at the door woke her. She blinked groggily, confused by how dark it was outside. It took her a long while to realize that she hadn't slept through to morning. It was still the same night, and some creature was hammering on her front door as if the world was ending.

"Hold on, hold on," she mumbled, pulling on her plush green velvet robe. "This had better be good." Vera lit the lamp on the table nearest the door to illuminate whoever might be there. "Who is it?" she called, remembering that she had aggravated a wolf not too long ago.

"Shady Hollow Message Service!" a voice chattered back. "Important message for Miss Vera Vixen!"

"Oh!" Vera thought of Philomena Ambler. Perhaps the bobcat had already uncovered some new information and sent it first by wingmail to the message service office and then to be delivered personally to Vera's door.

She opened the door to find a uniformed squirrel standing there.

"What time is it?" Vera asked.

"Half two!" the squirrel replied. "Message for you, Miss Vixen."

"Go ahead, please."

The squirrel then recited in a rapid-fire way, " 'Vera! Get down to the cop shop right now! Meade's got me behind bars and I ain't done nothing, and I told him you'd talk sense to him.' " The squirrel cleared his throat, adding in his normal tone, "Twenty cents, please. Collect message."

Vera was struggling to understand the words the squirrel had just conveyed. "Officer Ambler is here in Shady Hollow, and Meade arrested her?"

The squirrel twitched his nose, thinking hard. Then he said, "The message was sent by Lefty, who listed his occupation as 'honest citizen.' "

"Oh. Lefty. That makes more sense." Vera found a coin to

pay the messenger. Of course Lefty couldn't pay for it, since he was currently without cash, but—oh, no! What if Edward Springfield had finally reported the break-in and Lefty spilled the beans? The raccoon was not the most loyal creature at the best of times, and if he told the police that Vera paid him to sneak inside the Springfield house . . . well, that would make things very awkward with Orville.

Vera dressed in an outfit suitable for public view and hurried to the police station, worrying the whole time. The lights inside the station office were blazing, as were the tempers of the two bears yelling at each other.

"I was patrolling the streets, just like I'm supposed to do!" Chief Meade was insisting.

"Patrol shmatrol! You were snooping around my campaign office and had to make an arrest to justify why you were there!"

"Lefty is a criminal!" Meade yelled.

"Everyone knows that!" Orville shot back. "But that doesn't mean he was doing anything criminal just then!"

"Wait, wait, wait," Vera said, interrupting the argument. "Are you saying Lefty was arrested for breaking into Orville's campaign headquarters tonight?"

"Yes!" roared both bears.

"Oh, good," Vera said with a sigh.

"How is that good?" Meade asked.

"Uh, never mind. What did he take?"

"Nothing!" Lefty howled from his jail cell. "That's my whole point! I wasn't taking, I was giving!"

"Giving what?" she asked, hurrying to Lefty's cell.

"The latest flyers for the campaign," Lefty explained. "They finished printing real late, but I'm a night creature, so I do my volunteering in the wee hours."

"A likely story!" Meade snorted. "You're not a volunteer."

"Uh, he is, actually," Orville corrected. "And if you'd bothered to ask me instead of arresting Lefty and making me wake up and come down here in the middle of the night, you'd know that." Orville then turned to Vera. "How did you hear about this?"

"I got back from Highbank earlier this evening," said Vera, "and I'm *here* because Lefty sent a messenger squirrel to me when he got arrested. Which seems like a good idea, because someone needs to ask some sensible questions right now."

"Thank you!" Lefty grumbled.

"Okay." Vera pointed to Lefty. "You were in Orville's campaign office when?"

"At two o'clock this morning."

"And Chief Meade found you there and arrested you?"

"He didn't even ask me what I was doing there," Lefty whined. "Just cackled and cuffed me for breaking and entering. But I was only entering!"

Vera looked at Orville. "Seems to me that all you need to do is confirm nothing is missing from the office and that the new flyers are there."

"And that's what I will do," Orville replied. "But I had to rush down here when I heard that Meade had made an arrest! I was so sure he somehow caught the murderer we've been looking for." Orville grunted in disgust. "Should have known better."

Meade looked frustrated, which Vera could understand. He probably thought that catching Lefty on Orville's home turf, so to speak, would make Orville look bad. She looked over to the prisoner. "I still can't believe you're volunteering for a political campaign. What do you care about law and order?"

"Excuse me," the raccoon said, standing up on the jail cell's cot to gain enough height to look the bears in the eyes, "but politics touch everyone's lives, and I have a right and a responsibility to participate in the process. You cops! I bet you think I spend all my time moving merchandise that falls off the docks. I am not just a caricature!" Lefty rubbed his paws together. "Voting is for everybody!"

"You believe in universal suffrage?" Orville asked. "Even for felons?"

"Well, sure. Who knows more about what parts of the criminal justice system need reform?" Lefty countered.

Vera tipped her head, thinking about the raccoon's argument. *If Lefty ever runs for council, he might win.* "Well, we can debate voting rights in the morning. Now I think Chief Meade better unlock the cell and allow Lefty to go in peace."

Meade grumbled but did as Vera suggested.

"Orville and I will see Lefty safely home," she told Meade, "and tomorrow is a new day, so let's everybody act like it. No more one-upping or snooping or fighting about sign colors. Just a good, clean campaign. There are only a few days left!"

The bears looked at each other and grudgingly agreed.

Soon after, Vera and Orville escorted Lefty out of the police station. The raccoon took a deep breath when he got to the street. "Oh, freedom!" he said. "I knew you were the right fox to send for, Miss Vixen."

"You're lucky I got back to town when I did. And you owe me twenty cents for the collect message."

"Oh, sure. Pay you tomorrow . . . or the next day . . ."

"I didn't know you had keys to the campaign office, Lefty," Orville said then.

Lefty looked away. "Uh, technically . . . I don't."

"So you *did* break in?" Vera asked.

"Well, maybe, technically, I sort of did . . . but not for nefarious purposes! My purpose was entirely farious."

"I'm not sure that's a word," Orville noted.

"Skip the grammar," Vera said. "I'm definitely not writing up this little event for the paper; it makes everyone look bad. Lefty, can you please promise me that you'll go home and not break into any more places? And if you've broken into places in the past, *no one wants to hear about it*, okay?" she added with special emphasis.

"Sure thing, Miss Vixen," Lefty said. He peeled off near the river, heading toward his home.

Orville yawned. "I want to hear about Highbank, Vera, but I can't keep my eyes open. Breakfast at Joe's? You can tell me then."

"Sounds good," she agreed. "I'll definitely need some coffee to get through everything that happened to me upriver."

Chapter 17

Despite the disruption at the police station, Vera slept well for the rest of the night, and she hummed as she dressed for her breakfast date later that morning. She needed to get to work at the newspaper office, but she really wanted to talk with Orville first. Perhaps he would see something she had missed. She had gotten herself confused with one too many rats, and they *still* didn't know the identity of the decapitated creature discovered in the woods.

When Vera arrived at Joe's, she greeted Esme and then spotted Orville waving at her from a table in a corner of the diner. She hurried over to meet him, knowing Esme would soon appear with a full coffeepot. Vera glanced over the menu; the fall specials were all tempting. She was torn between maple-pumpkin pancakes with sunflower seeds and her favorite morning treat—a toasted sesame bagel with cream cheese, onion, and tomato. Orville said he was having the waffles with cinnamon whipped cream. By the time Esme returned to take their order, Vera had decided to go with the pancakes. Nothing says fall like special treats made with pumpkin.

After they placed their orders and Vera had rapturously sipped her coffee, Orville took her small paw in his two large ones and looked at her.

"Are you sure that you are all right?" he asked. "What went on in Highbank?"

Vera gave him a report that was mostly accurate. She did not want to alarm Orville, so she downplayed the moment when she landed in the pit.

"I fell in a hole and bruised my hindquarters as well as my dignity," she said, making light of the harrowing incident. "Thanks to that annoying wolf, I was none the worse for wear."

Orville looked concerned, but he seemed to accept her explanation.

"The worst thing about it all," Vera confessed, "is that I was so certain that Thomas was involved in this mess! But it's impossible unless he can meddle from beyond the grave. Officer Ambler was actually at the funeral, so there's no chance that Thomas arranged to have an empty casket put in the ground. Big Eddie confirmed the identity of the body that the Highbank police found, and Ambler's convinced that Eddie is the one responsible for Thomas's death, though she can't prove it."

"I've heard of Big Eddie," Orville said. "He's bad news and dangerous enough that the law in every town up and down the river knows his name. If Thomas Springfield crossed him, Eddie wouldn't think twice about making an example of the rat. Still, it's a little odd that he volunteered to identify the body. I mean, he'd be the prime suspect, so why help the cops? Unless he was taunting them . . ." He trailed off, looking out the window with a frown on his face.

"So what do I do now?" Vera asked. "I hate to think Dorothy has been driven out of her own home by this situation. I mean, let's put together the facts! She claims her husband was murdered, and then the body of a rat is discovered in the woods. Even though Dr. Broadhead may never be able to confirm it's Edward, who else could it be?"

"But then who is the rat who looks just like Edward?" Orville countered. "The only possible contender is the older brother, Thomas, but it can't be him. I don't want to bring up the other possibility," he added, his expression morose despite the cinnamon-dusted waffles he was eating, "but Dorothy has a history of some rather odd behaviors and remarks. What if she really did imagine it all?"

Vera sat back and twisted her whiskers, thinking hard. She drained her coffee mug and shook her head once. "No. Body in the woods. Blood in the foyer, on the rug, which I hope you believe me about now. We can't put those facts aside. A murder *was* committed. We need to solve the crime."

"You mean *I* need to solve the crime," Orville told her. "Meade and I, no matter how this election turns out. You've done great work, but without new clues, you'll just spin around in circles."

"I won't give up on Dot."

"No one's giving up. But you need to take a break from this case. Let me work, and if new information comes to light in the next day or two, you'll get another brilliant idea. I know how your brain works."

Vera sighed but dutifully turned her attention to the maple-pumpkin pancakes. It would be a crime to let them get cold. "A couple weeks ago, I volunteered to review all the voter registrations," she said. "It's for the town, not for a candidate, so I can do it without being biased. It's the only way I could think to help."

Orville slurped his coffee, then said, "Honestly, I wish Ms. Brocket had never found that body. Tell you one thing: whoever is responsible can't be from here. Any resident would know the area well enough to avoid the one part of the woods where everyone's digging! And yet here we are, and I have an unsolved murder right in the middle of my first political campaign. I'll be lucky if I get a single vote."

"You've got my vote," Vera told him, "and I'm sure everyone knows that you're doing your very best."

The couple finished their meal, both hurrying to get to their respective offices. Vera waved to Orville as he walked toward the police station, putting on a happier expression than what she felt inside.

As Vera told Orville over breakfast, she had promised to help the town hall workers verify voter registrations. It was a dull task that no one looked forward to, so Vera was the only volunteer who arrived at the building later that day.

"Oh, hullo, Miss Vixen," said one of several rabbits who worked there. "Come with me and I'll show you what needs to be done. We're a bit behind; the key to the storeroom got lost after the last big election, and no one realized until a couple weeks ago. We had to locate a spare, and until the room was opened yesterday, no one's been able to do a thing."

"Well, I'll do what I can," Vera said, wondering just how monumental the task would be.

"Don't worry, it's really not so bad. The goal is to keep the voter rolls updated so we don't accidentally disenfranchise someone. Usually discrepancies occur because a creature moved residences, or because they were underage during the last election and are now of age but forgot to submit the form letting us know. And deaths are the other thing: all removals due to death must be verified with an official notice on the approved list. There are forms for everything, though. Just follow the directions and you'll do fine."

The rabbit led Vera down to the storeroom, which looked like it hadn't been entered for the last *several* elections. Dust lay thick along the tops of oak filing cabinets. A few hanging lamps illuminated the space with a warm glow, and the chair at the worktable was padded in plush green velvet.

The rabbit hurried around, pulling piles of cards and stacked ledgers from various spots and placing them on the table. She quickly went through the instructions and told Vera to call if she had questions.

"But it's not difficult, just a bit tedious, dear. We thank you for your time—honestly, we're stretched pretty thin at the moment. This election is the biggest in years!"

Then the rabbit left, keeping the door propped open to the hallway. For the next few hours, Vera sat alone at the big worktable in the cool, faintly musty room, going through a pile of forms and stacks and stacks of registration cards.

She'd brought along a thermos of coffee and sipped from the mug every so often to keep her focus. This certainly was detailed work. It seemed inefficient to have to check and record all the information on a resident to ensure they weren't accidentally left off the rolls. But Vera knew that is the price one pays to live in a civilized free society.

Imagine a world where some voices are silenced, she thought. The woodland was a symphony of sounds—perhaps not all to one's liking but nevertheless part of the fabric of the forest world. To the creatures in Shady Hollow, silence meant danger.

That thought brought Vera right back to the case, even though she'd told Orville that she'd lay off it for a while. The niggling details just wouldn't leave her alone. She'd been so certain that Thomas was part of the answer. He'd been disowned by the Springfield family. Edward wouldn't talk about him. He'd crossed paths with criminals. He was like a ghost: physically gone but still haunting everyone.

"There's one extra rat," she muttered, leaning back in her chair. "One alive in the house whom we all call Edward. One buried in Highbank whom we all call Thomas. And one unearthed in the woods whom no one can name . . ."

She frowned. It all came back to that strange fact: the body in the woods had not just been killed but rendered unrecognizable. Why? Why, why, why?

"Rage? Hate? Or part of a plan?" Vera asked herself for the dozenth time. She shook her head. Without more information, she had no path forward.

"Ugh, Orville was right. We might be better off if that body had never been found."

Sighing, Vera kept at the task in front of her, working patiently, appreciating how her "done" stack grew over the hours. The issues she had to deal with here were simply mundane events of life that could confuse recordkeepers. Folks grew up, they got married, they moved, they died. It all had to be accounted for.

After sipping a bit more coffee, she reached for the next batch of cards. They were bundled and tied with twine along with a paper tag labeled *ML—Ward 4*. She untied the twine carefully since these registration cards were already brittle and yellowed with age.

She flipped through them, and a name jumped out: *Springfield*.

Eager to see if the voting records revealed anything new about the family she'd been researching, Vera read through the names and found several branches of the Springfield family tree, generations of dutiful citizens who'd cast their ballots every spring and fall as needed.

Then she got to *Springfield, Adora*. Well, that made sense— Adora's death was a recent event. Vera filled out the form for Adora, listing death as the reason for removal.

"'Supply official notice and confirm identity with supporting document,'" she read out loud from the instructions. "Okay, I've got a copy of the obituary here." She pinned the clipping to the form, pleased that her earlier work with the newspaper was helping here at the town hall. "Supporting document. Hmm." That meant Vera had to show there wasn't another Adora Springfield who might be confused with the deceased and thus unfairly removed from the rolls. It seemed a little silly in the case of such a well-known figure, but Vera sorted through the materials anyway.

Peering at one card, she matched the name on the registration form to that of the vital records: *Springfield, Adora (née Browne)*. "Here we go. Birth date, marriage date, and notices of offspring." The record would be more than sufficient in allowing Vera to confirm it was the same Adora.

Then Vera squinted at the card, staring at the notices of Adora's children. Edward's and Thomas's birth dates were duplicated. Same day, same month, same year. Was it a misprint?

A chill washed over her. It could be a misprint . . . or it could be perfectly accurate.

The answer was simple. Edward and Thomas were twins. Identical twins.

For a long moment, Vera simply sat there, too stunned to do anything at all.

Twins!

It was the only thing that made sense. It explained how one brother could perfectly impersonate the other. If the decapitated rat was Edward, then Thomas must have faked his death three years earlier to get away from Big Eddie, who'd been persuaded—somehow—that going along with Thomas's plan was more profitable than killing him outright. Now, three years later, Thomas murdered Edward and took his place in order to get the Springfield inheritance. However, he hadn't anticipated the unusual terms of the will. He'd never intended to fool Dorothy for more than a couple days. But when he found out that both spouses need to be alive to inherit, he'd been forced to change his plan and go with the risky move of continuing to impersonate Edward. It was difficult, and he couldn't do it perfectly because he didn't know more than the superficial details—hence his hazy responses at the wake. That's why the mine's forebeast, Clarence Hobbs, had been so alarmed at "Edward's" confusion over basic mining terms. And that was why "Edward" hadn't greeted Vera outside Mr. Fallow's office that first day . . . At that point, he hadn't known who Vera was!

She grabbed the documents, dashed out of the room, and yelled an apology to the town hall employees as she raced by.

"I'm borrowing a couple files, but I'll bring them back!" she called.

"Wait, wait!" a rabbit cried, startled.

But Vera was already outside, running toward the police station. When she arrived, she found Orville sitting at his desk, while Meade was nowhere to be seen.

"He's campaigning," Orville explained before seeing her expression. "What's happened?"

"Orville, I've got it! I mean, I think I've got it. Most of it. It's circumstantial, but—"

"Vera!" he cut in. "Take a breath! What are you going on about? What's all that material you've got?"

Vera hastily explained her theory and laid out the papers.

"But you said that's impossible, twins or not," Orville protested. "The Highbank police confirmed that Thomas died."

"Not exactly!" Vera said. "Philomena said the body was rather disfigured from being tossed in the river after death. Remember, it was Big Eddie himself who came forward—unasked!—to identify the body as Thomas. You said yourself it didn't really make sense for a criminal like him to do that . . . unless Thomas made it worth his while. Maybe Thomas struck a deal with Eddie to cover up for him. Some hapless traveler came to Highbank—say a male rat about Thomas's age. Thomas saw his chance. He killed the rat, and Eddie played along with the idea that the victim was really Thomas."

"For the inheritance?" Orville asked. "Eddie and Thomas might have waited ten years or more for that."

"I don't think Thomas told Eddie about that part of the plan. That was his private revenge—to hover near the family and wait for his opportunity. Remember how Professor Heidegger's house was broken into right before Shady Hollow first got the news that Adora was truly near death? I bet that was Thomas getting closer while he waited to strike."

"You sure?" Orville asked.

"I went to see Heidegger the day after the wake. Most of the books that got moved around were local histories and street directories—Thomas must have used them to study up on the creatures he'd need to know in his role as Edward. I remember him talking with one guest at the wake. He knew Stan Mortimer, probably from yearbook pictures, but he mostly asked questions and let Stan fill in the gaps. Plus the yearbooks would have revealed Edward and Thomas were identical twins. No wonder they were taken . . . Thomas was covering his tracks!

"Orville, we have to hurry," Vera told her beau finally. "If Thomas is still alive, this changes everything! Dot was right all along. Her husband is dead, and Thomas killed him. Now we just have to prove it."

"That's all very circumstantial, Vera." Orville's words were cautionary, but his tone was excited. "Maybe we can trip Thomas up. Make him confess to something that will let me arrest him."

"How can we take him by surprise?" Vera asked. "If he sees a cop, he'll be extra careful."

"Not if he thinks he's going to get exactly what he wants," Orville said.

"Like what?"

The big bear smiled, showing teeth. "Like Dorothy."

Chapter 18

Late that afternoon, when the light was growing golden, Vera and Orville advanced up the path to the Springfield house. On the sidewalk behind them, within earshot, stood Mr. Fallow with Dorothy, who was flanked by two squirrels in doctor's coats. She looked upset and nervous and skittish, and Vera felt much the same inside.

She raised her paw to knock three times on the heavy door. After a moment, she heard steps, and the door opened to reveal Edward's beleaguered expression. "Oh, Miss Vixen," he said, "I wasn't expecting you . . . or Deputy Braun." He frowned. "What's this all about? Have you seen Dotty lately? Is she ready to come home?"

"I'm afraid not," Vera said. She stepped aside so Edward could see Dorothy standing on the sidewalk. "That's why we're here."

"I don't understand," Edward said.

"After discussing the matter with Mr. Fallow and the hospital," Orville told him, "it's been decided that it might be best to place Mrs. Springfield in a medical facility for treatment. We all hoped that her, er, outburst would be forgotten. But she's adamant. And, after all, one can't stay at a bed-and-breakfast forever."

Edward's expression was somber, but Vera thought she detected a gleam in the rat's eyes. She said, "There's a bit of paperwork, of course. But if you could just fill out these forms, we can make sure Dorothy is safe and gets all the help she needs. Unless you object?"

"Oh, no." Edward shook his head. "I've tried over and over again to talk with her and to understand what she believes. So have our friends, all to no avail. I think what you're proposing is the right course of action."

Orville passed him a clipboard with several papers attached to it. "These are the forms, sir. The top one is spousal consent and power of attorney. The next one simply states that Dorothy is going to a facility run by Shady Hollow's hospital. And the last is just a municipal form asking for a lot of little details. Perhaps we should all go inside?"

"No, no, I can do it right here," the rat said, accepting the clipboard. "This is what needs to be done." He filled out all the forms with surprising speed and then offered the clipboard back to Orville. "Hope that's all, Officer. I suppose it's better if I don't speak to Dotty about this."

"*Doro*," Dorothy called from her spot on the sidewalk where she'd been listening keenly. "Edward always called me Doro. Always."

The rat shook his head sadly. "It really is getting bad. All right, then. If you all can escort her to the hospital, I'd be so grateful. I'll check in on her in a day or two, just to see she's getting what she needs."

Orville was scanning the forms, and he nodded with satisfaction. "Yes, this is more than sufficient."

"Oh, one more thing," Vera said. "I was just wondering . . . when I interviewed you for Adora's obituary, you said Thomas was the older brother."

The rat froze for the barest instant, unprepared for mention of this subject. But he said, slowly, "Yes."

"Fourteen minutes hardly seems to count as older. Edward was born fourteen minutes after his twin, named Thomas. That's what the vital record says . . . It's one of the few birth records that you didn't manage to steal or destroy, because it's been locked away in an unused storeroom with a missing key. But you worked hard to get rid of all other evidence of your existence . . . didn't you, Thomas?"

"You mean Edward," the rat said.

"No, you mean for us all to think you're Edward," Vera said coldly. "You snuck into Shady Hollow a couple weeks ago, hid out at Professor Heidegger's vacant house to get your bearings, and then came to this location late at night to kill your twin brother, Edward, and assume his identity. You intended to kill Dot the moment she returned from your mother's deathbed, too, because she's the one creature who'd be most likely to see through your act. But when you checked in with Mr. Fallow—probably after going through Edward's papers that first night—you discovered that the inheritance had an unexpected caveat. Both spouses have to be living, with their marriage intact, in order to inherit."

"This is madness," he said.

"Madness? That was your backup plan," Vera continued. "When Dorothy instantly realized you weren't Edward, you did everything you could to make her look mentally unsound. If no one believed her, you could keep up the facade."

"Stories," he declared. "Dorothy is delusional."

"No, she's not. And you knew that you were really in trouble the moment Edward's body was discovered in the woods. I remember something Orville said: any true local would know that patch of woodland is rumored to hold buried treasure. Folks have been digging in that area for the better part of a year to find it. But you're *not* a local, so you didn't know. If you'd chosen any other place to bury the body—after you beheaded it, to hide your brother's identity—your crime might never have been exposed. Poor Thomas. That's what you get for moving away from home."

"Do I have to listen to this, Officer?" Thomas asked, appealing to Orville.

"If it's not true, you have nothing to fear," Orville responded. "Of course, if it is true, that means you falsified an official document in the presence of an officer of the law. I can hold you on that charge alone."

"But you *can't* prove this fox's wild charge is true, can you?" the rat replied, now in a frosty, confident tone. Thomas smiled, looking around as though viewing a slightly amusing local theater production that had nothing to do with him. "It's a very interesting tale, to be sure, Miss Vixen. Worthy of Bradley Marvel, perhaps. But none of those so-called facts prove me a murderer. They don't even prove that I'm anyone other than Edward."

"When I was in your house for the interview, I checked the rug in the foyer," Vera told him. "Though you'd scrubbed and bleached the floor underneath, you couldn't remove the rug itself without drawing attention to it. And it still had blood on it, because you killed Edward in the foyer, perhaps right after he let you in."

"You say there's blood," Thomas said, now with a triumphal glint in his eyes, "but you can never prove it. And the deputy is well aware that I burned that old rug. I just didn't care for it."

"Maybe he missed a spot on the floor itself," Vera murmured to Orville.

Orville nodded. "You'd better let me inside to verify what I see in the foyer, Mr. Springfield."

"Oh, certainly." Thomas flung open the door to reveal the bare wood of the foyer. "See? Looks much tidier now, doesn't it? And that also means we've got only the word of this nosy reporter who *claims* she saw blood. Sounds like it's her word against mine."

"See this, Orville?" Vera pointed to the spots of damaged finish on the wood. "That's what happens when bleach interacts with wax on floorboards. Dorothy never keeps bleach in the house, so I bet you could go over to the general store here in Mirror Lake and learn that 'Edward' purchased a bottle of bleach that day."

"Bleach isn't blood," Thomas snapped.

Vera had to pull out her final card. "There's another witness who *did* see the rug in the foyer," she said. "Lefty was in the Springfield house a little after midnight on the day Dorothy made her accusation."

"Lefty? That little thief!" Orville grimaced. "Well, let's get him here to find out what he knows. Someone go fetch him—and don't say who's asking for him!"

One of the medical squirrels went to find Lefty. While they all waited, a crowd composed of neighbors and residents began to gather in front of the house. Sensing that something was up, they were quiet but watchful. It wasn't clear whose side they were on, if anyone's.

When Lefty arrived, Orville gestured for him to come up to the porch. "Now, Lefty. This is serious."

"Yes, Officer," Lefty said, shooting a glance at Vera.

"Were you in the Springfield house lately? Vera says you were."

"It's okay, Lefty," Vera added.

Lefty seemed a tad nervous when he looked at Orville, but he said, "Yes, I was in the Springfield house the evening after all the hullabaloo went on."

"Why?"

"Oh, I was just walking by. I . . . um . . . thought I saw a . . . flame through a window. Had to check it out as a . . . er . . . good citizen. Didn't want the house to burn down."

"So you let yourself into the house near midnight, through a window, taking care not to alert anyone, because you are a good citizen?"

"Um, yes."

"Go on," Orville growled.

"Well, when I got inside I was relieved to see that there was no fire. And it just so happened that I, er, kicked the rug in the foyer, and I saw that the floor had been recently scrubbed clean. Bleached. As if a creature had worked very hard to remove a bloodstain."

"Speculation," Thomas said loftily.

"Go on," Orville repeated.

"Well, I was going to leave. But then I heard someone moving about, and I thought it might be a thief. So I snuck toward the sound and saw *him* standing in the kitchen." Lefty pointed to Thomas. "At the time, I thought it was Edward."

"What was he doing in the kitchen at that hour?" Vera asked.

"He wasn't thieving anything. I'd know," Lefty admitted. "He was just making a peanut butter sandwich."

"Midnight snack," Thomas added. "I've done that for years. Dorothy can confirm it if she chooses to."

Dorothy stood, shaking like a leaf, a parade of emotions crossing her face. "It's true," she murmured. "Edward did like a late meal, usually just before bed, but sometimes he'd even get up in the middle of the night. He told me he used to sneak out of his bed and creep past his parents' door so that he could eat some jam or cheese or bread in peace."

"Something his twin would know," Vera noted.

Thomas shrugged.

"Wait!" Dorothy looked at Lefty and asked, "Did you say a peanut butter sandwich?"

"Yeah. It was Ms. Muncie's peanut butter, with that bright red label. Can't miss it."

Something like triumph flashed in Dorothy's eyes. "Edward was allergic to peanuts! I never had anything containing peanuts in the house."

Vera gasped. "Ambrosius Heidegger had a lot of Ms. Muncie's products in his house! Remember, Orville? Heidegger reported food stolen . . . which occurred at the same time the mystery occupant destroyed the old yearbooks on his shelves."

Vera thought it very likely that Thomas took the food he liked with him when he absconded from Heidegger's tree and came to the Springfield house.

"Who cares who's got what in whose pantry?" Thomas snapped. "Dotty's coming up with completely absurd excuses that are totally unprovable! I like peanut butter and have always eaten it."

"Sun Li can tell you all about *Edward's* reaction to peanuts," Dot said. "Once when Edward and I went to dinner at the Bamboo Patch, he dipped one of his pot stickers in my sauce. A tiny amount of sauce, but there were peanuts in it, and Edward nearly stopped breathing. Sun Li rushed out of the kitchen and saved him! Thank goodness the chef is a former surgeon. If you ask, I'm sure he'll remember."

The police bear turned to a squirrel wearing a messenger uniform. "Go to Sun Li's house behind the Bamboo Patch. Tell him we need his testimony right away. Don't tell him what about!" Orville added. "He must be unbiased."

The squirrel saluted, dashing up the nearest tree and then rocketing toward Shady Hollow.

It did not take long for the squirrel to return with Sun Li in tow. The panda was carrying a black leather bag, apparently thinking that his medical skills were called for. But once he saw the crowd of folks standing around, he slowed, looking puzzled.

"What's all this?" he asked upon reaching Orville and the rest of the group. "I was told there is an emergency!"

"There sure is," Orville said, "but not the kind you're think-ing. What I need to hear from you, Mr. Sun, is whether you remember an incident in your restaurant concerning Dorothy and Edward Springfield."

Sun Li glanced at Dot and said, "Remember it? Of course! I assume you're referring to the time Edward ate some of Dot's peanut sauce—less than a spoonful but more than enough to send him into anaphylactic shock. It was very lucky that I'd recently restocked my medical supplies. I administered the drug needed to counter Edward's immediate symptoms and then monitored him to ensure that he wouldn't have another reaction. We had to carry him out of the restaurant. I didn't want him anywhere near peanuts or peanut oil after I found out he was allergic."

"So in your expert opinion," Orville asked carefully, "Edward Springfield could not eat any amount of peanuts—say, a peanut butter sandwich—safely?"

"Goodness, no. That would kill him." Sun Li realized what he'd said and abruptly looked at Dot once more. Only then did the panda register that "Edward" was in custody.

"I have a question for you as a former doctor," Vera said then, stepping up. "Consider the case of identical twins. Is it possible for one twin to have such an allergy, but the other twin not to have it?"

After a thoughtful pause, Sun Li nodded. "Yes, quite possible. Allergies are rarely congenital. They have to do with exposure and how a body reacts."

"Well, then." Vera looked to Orville. "That should settle it."

The deputy said, "Thomas Springfield, I'm bringing you in on suspicion of murdering Edward Springfield, your twin brother. The circumstantial evidence is more than enough to put you in a holding cell." Orville grabbed Thomas by the foreleg, and the rat struggled for half a second before realizing just how futile physical resistance would be.

Thomas preferred other methods, anyway. He yelled, "I want an attorney! Get Fallow here, he's the family lawyer!"

"I am here, sir," Mr. Fallow said. He stepped forward, looking dignified and calm—a welcome counterpoint to the general nervousness of the crowd.

"You're my lawyer! Stop this yokel from shackling me and dragging me to a cell."

Mr. Fallow looked at Thomas for a long moment, then removed his glasses, which he polished slowly. Not until he put them back on his nose did he reply, "I am sorry, sir. I must recuse myself. For, as you say, I am the attorney for the Springfield family, and it seems there may be a conflict of interest at play, considering the facts, the accusation, and the differing accounts between Mrs. Springfield and yourself . . . and, indeed, your actual identity."

Orville nodded to Mr. Fallow, satisfied that there would be no last-minute legal shenanigans. He gripped Thomas's paws hard as he adjusted a pair of cuffs on the enraged rat. "You'll find our cells are quite decent," Orville said. "Move along. The sooner I get you to the station, the sooner you can get out of the cuffs."

"And behind bars!" Thomas huffed.

"Yes, that is the general concept of jail," Orville agreed, his tone mild now that he had a suspect in custody.

The crowd watched in silence as Orville hauled Thomas off to the police station.

"Oh, my," Dorothy said, breaking the spell. She nearly sagged as her knees wobbled in relief. "He's finally gone. I can go home."

"I'll walk you up the steps," Vera told her, offering a paw to help Dorothy walk more steadily. "You must be very keen to get inside."

"Oh, yes. And no! After weeks of that impostor lurking in the house, it'll need a good cleaning. And possibly a smudging."

Looking at all the concerned faces, Vera said, "I expect that if you ask around for sage, your neighbors will pile more on your front porch than you'll know what to do with."

The walk was made easier by Mr. Fallow, who paced on the other side of Dorothy and held out his elbow to offer an escort.

"What led you to the conclusion that the brothers were twins?" Mr. Fallow asked Vera.

"To tell the truth, I lucked into the actual evidence. But I think that, subconsciously, I must have known it was the only possible explanation." Vera remembered the day she walked to the shore of Mirror Lake and saw a rat fishing from the pier. She recalled how he'd waved to her with his upside-down reflection mimicking the move. "It was a wild idea—a secret twin who managed to erase his existence until his moment of revenge. But consider the facts: Dorothy insisted her husband was dead, and yet we all saw a figure who looked exactly like Edward. It was either magic or twins. And I don't believe in magic! It's impossible."

"And once we eliminate the impossible, whatever remains, however improbable, must be the truth," Mr. Fallow quoted. "Wise words."

"I found the actual evidence in the town hall. Luckily," Vera said, "I needed to be nonpartisan in my volunteering for this election, so I opted to help with voter registrations. And part of that process is retiring deceased voters' names. I searched for Adora's information, which included birth records for her children. It was the one place Thomas never thought of; otherwise he surely would have destroyed the records."

"Just like the yearbooks at Professor Heidegger's!" Mr. Fallow shook his head. "What a remarkable capacity for evil Thomas had. Just think if he'd used his intelligence for a more noble purpose."

They walked up the path to the Springfield house. Vera remembered the exact scene from the day when she and Mr. Fallow had run up to find Dorothy standing on this lawn, with the mirror image of Edward Springfield across from her. How long ago that seemed, and yet it had been only a couple weeks!

Inside the large house, Dorothy walked around lighting lamps and candles. She examined each room with a sharp, careful eye.

"Dusty, dusty, dusty," she said, clucking her displeasure. "I've never let this house go for so long without a cleaning."

Vera looked around and saw a bit of disarray but not much worse. Thomas might've been a murderer, but he wasn't messy. "It's not so bad," she ventured to say.

"Oh, you're trying to cheer me up. But I know that scoundrel didn't care for this place properly . . . not like a real Springfield would. Look!" Dorothy pointed to a table by a window, where the silver lily lamp stood with its mismatched shade. "That lamp had a different shade, a pretty glass one with lots of little green bits. Now there's just a cheap linen shade from the spare room! Thomas must have broken the lampshade and hid his foul deed. Just like all his other foul deeds! Oh, I loved that lamp."

Vera bit her tongue, deciding to keep Lefty's name to herself . . . After all, the damage was done. No sense in dragging up the raccoon's clumsy error. Especially since his witnessing of the peanut butter sandwich provided the final clue to prove Thomas a fraud!

"I'm just so glad this is over," Dorothy said with a sigh.

Vera nodded but then noticed the bare spot on the foyer floor—an ugly reminder of what had happened in this house. Even with Thomas in jail, was the ordeal over? Could it ever be truly over?

Chapter 19

Thomas's arrest provided the residents of Shady Hollow and Mirror Lake with no end of gossip, and this dovetailed with the final few days of campaigning before the election. Signs popped up in yards and banners hung from doorways, especially bright red and yellow ones for the police chief race. Vera silently counted the signs as she walked through town, but it was impossible to tell who had the edge.

Election Day dawned bright and sunny. The cold snap in the air was more invigorating than harsh, and Vera thought the weather boded well for voter turnout. She dressed hurriedly and bypassed her small kitchen on the way out the door. She'd grab a bite at Joe's later, but first she wanted to get to the polls to interview folks as they performed their civic duty.

At the central polling place, located at the town hall itself, she interviewed Moira Chitters, one of Howard's more-precocious offspring. Moira had attempted to cast a vote this morning but was prevented from doing so when the poll workers noticed her youthful expression beneath her grandmother's wide-brimmed hat. They informed Moira that children were not permitted to vote.

"But I *want* to!" Moira protested even as she was being escorted away from the ballot box.

"Not till you're a bit older, dear," one of the poll workers said kindly.

Vera knelt down to comfort the young mouse and asked her for a comment on the state of local politics and on voting in general. "I should get a vote," Moira insisted. "I live here, too!"

"That's a good point," Vera said, writing in her notebook. "What do you think needs changing here in Shady Hollow?"

"We could use more slides at the playground," Moira said, "and the rope swings into the river are just not long enough."

"You should go to the next town council meeting," Vera suggested. "Anyone can speak at those."

"Oh! Really?" Moira had a glint in her eyes as she hurried home.

After interviewing a few more locals, Vera got in line to vote herself. In the booth, she needed only a moment to mark her choices. She pressed extra hard on her pencil when circling Orville's name.

Afterward, she passed through the exit door to find a long table set up nearby, with a number of creatures standing around it. "Good morning, voter!" a squirrel called to her, gesturing her over.

"What's this?" Vera asked, sniffing the air above the table.

It held an assortment of humble little cakes that smelled delicious.

"It's election cake, of course!" the squirrel replied. "Oh, maybe you've never voted in Shady Hollow before, Vera. This is a tradition in all the towns up and down the river. There's a cake committee for each ward, and we get together to bake these little cakes. We sell them only on Election Day . . . and you aren't allowed to buy one until you've left the polling booth."

"Now that's an incentive I can understand," Vera said, glancing at the line forming behind her as folks left the polls and stepped right up to the cake table, eager to be rewarded for their civic duty. The cakes were redolent with spices: cinnamon and cloves and nutmeg and the sweet aroma of molasses under it all. "How much?"

"Twenty-five cents, please," the squirrel told her. "Enjoy!"

Vera took her cake, which was wrapped in a red-gingham cloth napkin, and smiled. She fully intended to enjoy her treat.

The polls closed at six o'clock in the evening, just as the town residents left their businesses and schools and returned home for a hearty dinner. The temperature had taken a sharp plunge as the sun set, and the chill in the air strongly encouraged creatures to bundle up and find a warm place to relax.

Vera and Lenore got together for a meal at Joe's Mug. It was packed with folks gathered to dine and chat and guess the results of the races. Vera was too nervous to eat much of anything, and she wondered over and over again if she ought to have done something differently. Should she have told Orville not to run? Should she have quit her job to direct his campaign? Should she have a piece of pumpkin pie, and if so, should she have it with vanilla or maple ice cream? It was all very fraught.

Then a rabbit opened the diner door. Though folks had been coming and going constantly, now they all turned expectantly.

"Results are in!" the rabbit cried out, scarcely slowing as he delivered the message to each business. "Results are in! The mayor will read the results in the town square at eight o'clock!"

"Well, that's it. Let's get moving so we can get close to the stage." Lenore ruffled her feathers, then smoothed them down.

"Oh, I'm not sure I can listen. I'll stay here," Vera said.

"Nonsense. You're an intrepid reporter; you can't be spooked by a little tension. And, anyway, Orville's got this."

"You don't know that."

"I never had a doubt. Now come along, Vera, or I'll tell your beau that you were going to desert him in his hour of triumph!"

"Now that's just mean."

"Yes, I know." Lenore cawed with delight, and Vera was reminded of just why she and the raven got along so well.

A large crowd had gathered in the town square and was chattering excitedly. Orville met up with Vera and Lenore, and the trio stood together to await the results. This was Shady Hollow's most interesting race in several years, and folks were not going to wait for tomorrow's *Herald* to learn the results. They wanted to know *now*.

The mayor read off the results in reverse order of their importance to Vera.

"The winner of the comptroller position is Nancy Chitters . . . again. Congratulations, Nancy . . .

"The race for town clerk goes to Mariana Beckenbauer . . . We look forward to your service, Ms. Beckenbauer!"

Polite applause followed each announcement, but it was clear folks were waiting for the big finish.

"And finally . . ." The mayor paused to take a long sip of water, and Vera ground her teeth at the obvious tease.

"Get on with it!" someone yelled from the crowd, and a general roar confirmed the sentiment.

"All right, all right. In the race for chief of police, the result is . . . Orville Braun, by one hundred and twelve votes. Congratulations, Deputy Braun . . . that is, *Chief* Braun!"

Vera squealed with excitement and joy. More than a hundred votes ahead! That was a landslide! "Oh, Orville, you did it!" She threw her arms around him. "I'm so proud of you!"

Orville hugged her tightly, saying in his gruff voice, "Couldn't have done it without you."

"Speech!" someone called out. "Speech!"

The cry was taken up by the crowd, and Vera said, "I think you'll have to go up there and say a few words. They won't take no for an answer."

"Oh, bother," Orville grunted. But he waved to the crowd and climbed the short staircase to join the mayor at the podium.

"Ah, here's our new police chief," the mayor shouted. "The floor is yours, Orville."

Orville looked over the crowd and seemed rather overwhelmed for a moment. But then he straightened up and said, "Thank you. Quite honestly, thank you to everyone who voted for me. It means a lot to have your trust. And for those of you who didn't vote for me . . . well, I'll earn your trust. I mean to serve Shady Hollow as best I can and to uphold the law, just as Chief Meade has done for so long. He's a fine public servant, too, and even now, he's at the station, working his shift just like he should. I want to thank him for his many years of dedication to our town."

Vera started clapping, and others soon joined. Feet stomped in approval. It was a good speech, short and sweet. Orville waved once more, yelled a final thank-you to the crowd, and left the stage as fast as he could.

In anticipation of this outcome, Orville's campaign team had planned a victory party at his headquarters. It felt like most of the town decided to attend. Joe Junior had set up the catered food—mostly sandwiches and snacks and pies that were being doled out as fast as Joe and Esme and Lucy could slice them. A band in the corner played music that the happy guests were all shouting over, adding to the din.

Vera and Lenore stood to one side, munching on their favorite treats while watching the party.

"Turned out pretty well," Lenore admitted. This was about as cheerful as the raven ever allowed herself to be. "And now Meade will get to spend even more time fishing, so it all works."

Orville approached Vera, bowing. "Care to dance?" he inquired.

Vera smiled and put her paw in his as they walked onto the makeshift dance floor. Orville was a good dancer, and he and Vera whirled around the floor to the beat of the music. She couldn't help beaming with joy, delighted with her beau, her town, and her life in general.

Just then, Meade rushed into the room, his eyes wild.

The music faltered, the trumpeter playing an inadvertent solo until he realized his bandmates had all stopped and were staring in shock at the sudden appearance of a bear—and not just any bear, but the losing bear of the day's race. The arrival jarred everyone into silence.

"Oh, no," Vera muttered. "What's he up to?" She feared that Meade, not reacting well to his loss, might have gotten some foolish notion into his head. Perhaps he was going to make a scene and embarrass himself or make life difficult for Orville.

But the older bear skidded to a halt well before he reached Orville. Panting heavily, he burst out, "It's all gone wrong! You've got to come quick!"

"What's going on?" Orville asked, worry on his face. "What's gone wrong? Was there a miscount?"

"No, it's much worse than that!" Meade shouted. "I went to check on the prisoner since he'd been quiet all evening, and when I got there . . . the cell was empty. Thomas has escaped!"

Chapter 20

To say the scene turned to chaos would be an understatement. Creatures who'd overheard the initial outburst shouted in alarm; the rest of the partygoers were already murmuring and muttering about the two bears who'd just fought in the race for police chief. Vera glanced around, noticing the agitation of the crowd and the shift in mood.

Orville was pumping Meade for more details about the escape, pointedly asking if the chief had fallen asleep and if the cell keys were all accounted for.

Vera pushed herself between them. "Stop it, both of you! None of that matters now. If Thomas is at large, we've got to get to Dorothy!"

"Before *he* does," Orville added grimly.

"She left here for home less than half an hour ago," Lenore said. "She might not have arrived yet."

"Lenore, if you fly, you can find her much faster than any of us can get to her."

"But in the dark," Lenore said uncertainly, "my eyes aren't so good. If she's under tree cover, I might miss her entirely."

"Heidegger," Orville said suddenly.

Of course, Vera thought. Orville was a quick thinker, despite his sometimes-lumbering manner. The owl would have no problem searching for Dorothy even in the darkest night. "That's perfect. Where is he?"

Vera scanned the crowd, but Orville chose a more direct method, roaring Heidegger's name over the rest of the creatures' heads.

An awkward silence descended.

"Heidegger, get over here!" Orville called again. "You're not in trouble," he added—a useful note for those discovering that a bear wants a word.

A moment later, the owl rose on buff-colored wings, which sent an instinctive chill through the hearts of some of the smaller guests. He settled down before Orville, ruffling his feathers. "I say, sir, there's no need to shout, especially on such a festive occas—"

"Listen up, Heidegger," Orville cut in. "I have a mission for you."

The owl perked up, his chest puffing out. "A mission?"

"Yes. You must fly to Mirror Lake, to the Springfield house. If you see Dorothy Springfield on the way, fly down to her and let her know that Thomas has escaped. And *don't* leave her side

until I get there to relieve you. Meade and I will come as fast
as we can."

Heidegger saluted with one wing tip. "Consider it done!"
He left the victory party and took flight in almost the same
moment as when he reached the outside. He lifted into the
sky on silent wings and was lost in the gloom a moment later.

"All right," Orville said. "Meade, let's get moving. Thomas
is tricky, but he can't deal with both of us."

"You . . . you want me along?" Meade asked.

Orville gave a grunt. "Just said that, didn't I?"

"I'm coming, too," Vera said.

"And me." Lenore raised her wing. "We'll need all the help
we can find. The woods are thick between here and Mirror
Lake, and we don't know what route Thomas is taking to get
there."

"If he's going there at all," Vera added, suddenly doubting
her own guess. "Maybe he ran for the river to steal a boat and
get out of the area before dawn."

"No way," Lenore said. "He's got revenge in his heart. Now
that he can no longer pretend to be Edward, there's no need
to keep Dorothy alive. He's going to kill her. Especially after
everything he's done to get to this point."

"Less talk," Orville growled. "More action."

"*That's* why you won," Meade said.

And with that statement, the two bears charged out of the
building, leaving bewildered partygoers behind.

Vera and Lenore did not stop to enlighten anyone beyond
offering Joe Junior the briefest version of events. "Keep folks
here if you can," Vera added. "Thomas is a danger to anyone
he encounters!"

"And what does that mean for you?" the younger Joe asked,

but his words were directed to empty air, because fox and raven had already left.

The cold night folded around Vera—a shock after the cozy warmth of the victory party. She dashed along the street with Lenore flying just overhead. "Direct route?" Vera called to her friend.

"You take the main path," Lenore cawed back. "I'll fly over a wider area and let you know if I see anything funny. Be careful!"

Vera nodded, but how can a creature be careful in such a situation? Dorothy was in danger and didn't even know it!

Vera raced through the dark woods. Lanterns hung from branches every so often, at regular intervals—not so much for illumination, more as reassurance that travelers were going the right way. Vera felt grateful for the marked path.

However, about halfway along, Vera came across a smashed lantern. Glass lay in pieces on the pathway. Ahead was only darkness.

"Lenore!" she called to the sky.

A moment later, the raven landed in front of her, a patch of black against the already-black scene. "All the lamps ahead are out," Lenore reported. "I can see where the lights end. But any creature can find their way eventually. What's his game?"

"To slow us down, maybe," Vera guessed, "or this is how he captured Dot because she couldn't see him in the darkness. Lenore, fly directly to the house and see if any windows are uncovered. When I get there, I'll signal. Let me know what you find."

"Will do." The raven took off again.

Vera moved more cautiously now, not certain what was going to happen. Thomas easily could be lurking behind one of these trees. Perhaps he'd allowed Orville and Meade to run by only to lie in wait for Vera, the most persistent of the investigators.

She reached the Springfield house at last. It loomed dark and silent in the night. The figures of the police bears were on the front lawn, joined by the shape of an owl and then the shape of a raven.

Vera hurried up to them. "No sign of Dorothy?"

"Nothing," Orville said grimly. "But we saw one set of tracks—rat prints—and also signs of something being dragged. The tracks go right up to the front steps. I'm guessing Thomas waited in the woods for Dorothy to walk by and—" He mimed hitting someone over the head.

"He dragged her all the way here." Vera gasped. "They're both inside!"

"All the doors are locked and all the windows are bolted," Meade said. "Lenore thought she saw a light flickering inside, but then it went out."

"If we break a window to get in, he'll hurt Dorothy. She's a hostage now." Orville looked at the house with a frown.

Vera nodded. "You two stay here. If Thomas is watching, he'll see you dithering and think he's safe. Lenore and Ambrosius, keep flying in circles. If he tries to escape, you've got to give a signal!"

"What about you?" Orville asked.

"I'm going to find some way in," Vera vowed. "Dorothy isn't going to face this creature alone."

Vera left the group and edged around the house, looking for a route inside that Thomas might have missed. Knowing Orville and Meade already checked the windows and doors, she skipped them, instead focusing on the lower part of the house, where the side gardens grew thick. Perhaps a basement or a root cellar connected to the main house.

What was that story Parson Conkers told at Adora's funeral? Yes! Vera remembered. After a terrible storm, a huge tree fell and blocked the front of the house, but Adora simply used the storm-cellar door.

Under the heavy branches of a yew, Vera saw a corner of wood that seemed unnatural. Diving below the yew, she found the side of a storm-cellar door, which was now overgrown to such an extent that it was hidden entirely.

"Hello," she murmured. The slanted planks of the door were solid, and the door was held in place by a lock. But when Vera tugged at the lock, it dissolved into a heap of rusted flakes.

She pried the door open and slipped into the dank space below.

Vera found herself in a dug-out basement with a dirt floor. It held several crates and many shelves, some filled with preserved food in jars. She made her way to the staircase and crept up slowly, praying that the steps wouldn't creak and betray her.

After what seemed like an hour, she reached the top. Easing the door open, she emerged on the ground floor. She heard a few slight noises but couldn't tell what they meant or where exactly they were coming from.

She crept through the dim rooms, wishing she had a light.

When a floorboard creaked under one paw, she froze. Had Thomas heard it? Was he close enough to realize he wasn't alone?

After a few tense moments, she continued on.

At the doorway to the living room, the air behind her changed.

"Why, good evening, Miss Vixen."

She whirled to see Thomas standing there. "Where's Dorothy?" Vera demanded.

"Upstairs, tied up. I have plans for her, and I don't want to rush things."

Thomas smiled at Vera, looking like a sinister version of the rat in the painting above the fireplace. "You really are a nosy reporter. I should have known you'd get in here somehow."

"The storm-cellar door," she said shortly. "The one we all heard about at Adora's funeral. You should have checked the lock on it. Rusted all the way through." She paused, then added with a tiny bit of spite, "Dorothy would have noticed if she'd had any chance at all to spend time at home."

"If you're so smart, why'd you sneak into a murderer's house all alone?" From the folds of his clothing Thomas pulled out a large wicked-looking knife.

"My friends are just outside," Vera told him in what she hoped was a forceful tone.

"Ah, but they're not in here, are they?" Thomas approached her, moving with a slinky, stealthy gait that was hard to evade. He seemed to always be one step closer than before, no matter how Vera tried to maneuver away. "You know, this is the knife I killed Edward with. Very reliable."

"Was it the knife you used to kill whoever is lying in the Highbank cemetery? The rat Big Eddie passed off as you?"

Thomas nodded, smiling wide. "I'm flattered, really, that you went to Highbank to search for clues. I wasn't sure you'd pick up the hints I was offering. So difficult to know how thick to lay it on. You took a few days, but you got the boat at last, so I knew I could put the next part of my plan in motion. I messaged Big Eddie with a few instructions, and you got his note, just as you were intended to. That idiot wolf was the only wild card. How was I supposed to guess that he'd be so puppy-doggish as to follow you around a murder investigation?"

"I'm lucky he did," Vera admitted.

"The blind alley at the Highbank cemetery was supposed to have been enough for you," Thomas said, anger twisting his features. "You were supposed to give up on hunting down Thomas Springfield because he was dead. But you just wouldn't let it go."

He raised the knife.

"You're the one who planned revenge for twenty years!" Vera squeaked as she dodged away. "Talk about not letting go!"

"It wasn't revenge," Thomas told her, again preparing to pounce and whip the knife at her face. "It's the money! I want the money that is my due."

"You don't deserve money just for being born," she gasped out, then she turned tail and ran up the stairs.

"You can't get away!" Thomas called, moving after her. "You think I'll let you slip free after ruining all my hard work?"

"If only you had that work ethic when it comes to honest labor."

"I tried," Thomas said. "I really did. Took jobs, toiled like anyone else. It just didn't ever work out. I played a few too many games with the wrong folks and got into too much debt."

"Like Big Eddie. You owed him."

"A lot," Thomas confirmed. "He was going to kill me, but I managed to persuade him that there was a better way. You were pretty close to the truth, Vixen. By chance I met a vagrant coming through to Highbank from the southern forest. I ran into him before he was ever seen in town. I offered him a place to sleep in exchange for a few odd jobs . . . and that night, I killed him and brought the body to Big Eddie. We dressed the body in my clothes, and I slipped my wallet into his pocket. Big Eddie cut a few toes off the corpse to match mine. See, I'd already been taught that Big Eddie is serious about money."

"And Eddie tossed the body into the river while you skedaddled."

"Yup. He knew how to time it so the body would be found well after it was made known that he was 'looking' for me. He even went to the cops to make sure they thought the corpse was me. After that it was just waiting. I did some work for Big Eddie while I bided my time and checked in on the progress of my dear old mum."

"And when she got very sick, you made your move."

Thomas shrugged. "Might as well tell you since you won't be leaving here. Not alive, anyway."

All this time, Vera had been slowly moving down a second-floor hallway, toward a big double staircase. At the other end of the hallway stood a framed mirror. Thomas stalked her relentlessly, not taking his gaze off her. And that was how he missed what Vera saw.

Vera screamed and pointed at a pale wavering shape behind Thomas. "Edward?" she gasped out.

Thomas looked by instinct and froze for a split second, staring at the image: his brother, Edward, dressed in a suit and carrying a knife, his expression twisted with fear and hate.

Then Thomas laughed, realizing the image was nothing more than his reflection in the giant mirror.

"Good trick, Vixen," he growled, "but not good enou—"

He went silent as a large cooking ladle impacted his head. The knife dropped from the rat's nerveless paw, and he crumpled to the floor.

Dorothy stepped out of the shadowed alcove where Vera had moments before noticed her hiding. She held up the implement. "I use this every time I make a vegetable soup. Never thought it would be a weapon. That was a perfect distraction."

"I did what I could," Vera said. "I figure Thomas secretly might be afraid that his brother will want to take revenge from beyond the grave."

Dorothy skirted around the edge of the hall to avoid the unconscious Thomas. "It took me a little while to get untied from those ropes! How long will he be out?"

"Long enough for the police to take care of him. And this time he won't escape."

A few short minutes later, both Meade and Orville entered the house and tied Thomas up tightly with his own rope.

"Back to the jail cell," Meade declared. "And I'll set a watch all night. I'm glad he's not dead; he needs to stand trial."

"Here *and* in Highbank," Orville added. "There's a body up there that needs accounting for. And Thomas might just be the key to taking down Big Eddie. This could end up being a very good day for justice in the woodlands."

"Quite a start to your run as chief," Vera said.

"I hope the rest of my run isn't so eventful. Now let's get this miserable creature back to his jail cell. And tomorrow we'll sort out all the details." Orville looked at Vera meaningfully. "Such as how you knew Lefty was here that night."

Vera smiled weakly. "That will be an interesting conversation."

"Uh-huh," Orville agreed. "One that will require a lot of coffee and a lot of pie to endure."

Epilogue

Vera spent a few long days and nights working feverishly on her story for the newspaper. She made sure to thank the authorities in Highbank and Shady Hollow and put in a special note of appreciation for Ms. Boatwright's excellent reference work. BW Stone was so eager for the draft that he couldn't even sit in his chair. He paced a tight square in his office, puffing madly on his cigars and yelling at anyone who passed his door to "Check on that Vixen!" and hurry her along.

When Vera finally arrived to give her final draft to BW, he practically snatched it out of her paws. He exchanged his cigar for a big red pen and set to reviewing the piece, making lots of scribbled comments and swooping marks for the proofreaders. At the end, he sat back in his chair, sighing heavily.

"What a scoundrel," he said, his expression rather stunned. Then his eyes brightened. "Let's get some pictures to run with this on the front page. We're going to need extra print runs for this issue!"

He summoned the proofreader—a young rabbit with black fur, very long ears, and a good eye for typos. BW gave instructions on what he wanted and then set the rabbit bounding off to carry out the orders.

"All right, Vixen," BW told her then. "Good work. Take today and tomorrow off, and try not to stumble over any more corpses while you're out."

"Yes, sir!" Vera agreed.

By evening, everyone in town was reading Vera's article and chattering about the murderer in their midst. Thankfully, as a hopeful counterpoint, in a corner of the front page was a small article titled "Silver Mine Heiress to Return Home by End of Year." Hazel Springfield, the daughter of Edward and Dorothy, had booked passage on a ship as soon as she got word of what happened so that she could be reunited with her mother. Vera was glad for that and hoped the New Year would be a good one for them both.

All in all, Vera was done with excitement for a good long time. She spent her day off in her own den, enjoying a pot of tea and reading one of the many books waiting for her on her shelf.

The next morning, she rose very early, because Orville was due at the town hall for his swearing-in ceremony as the new chief of police. By tradition this ceremony was performed at sunrise on the Sunday after an election. No one especially liked this tradition, but since it was enshrined in the town ordinances from the very founding of Shady Hollow, it was respected.

With bleary eyes, the mayor swore in the winners of the recent races, who all raised sleepy limbs and recited the pledge to serve in somber tones. The exception to this was Mariana Beckenbauer, the oriole who would serve as town clerk. She looked wide-awake as she trilled her pledge to file all papers correctly and with promptitude. Vera tried not to resent early birds, but sometimes it was difficult.

Orville received his new badge, which looked exactly like his old badge except that it said CHIEF instead of DEPUTY and was brilliantly shiny with newness. After the ceremony concluded, most of the participants headed toward a table set with coffee and pastries. But Orville escorted Vera outside, intent on spending some time alone.

They strolled down the main thoroughfare, enjoying the hushed scenes of empty streets and sidewalks and the buildings all quiet and sleepy except for the occasional glow from a window.

At Nevermore Books, light streamed from the doorway. "Huh," said Vera. "It looks like Lenore is already at work."

They knocked and stepped inside. The raven fluttered down from her office at the top level. When asked, she told them she'd stayed at the store overnight. "Unpacking a big shipment of gift books that I couldn't deal with while all the Marvel nonsense was going on. Thankfully that's taken care of and I can work on my new displays!"

"Looks good, Lenore," Orville said, taking in the view. The bookshop certainly looked a lot more spacious without all the chairs set up for the event.

"Why, thank you, *Chief* Braun." The raven nodded at Orville's shiny metal badge, suitably impressed. "Got that this morning, did you? What's your first order of business?"

"Walking my beat," he replied, "which is what I did before anyway."

"But this time, I'm walking with him," Vera added, curling one paw around the shaggy limb of her beau.

"Lucky him." Lenore winked. "Have a good time. And don't wander too far. Snow's on the way."

Despite Lenore's warning, Vera saw no evidence of oncoming winter other than the increasingly bare branches above her head. The morning sun burned in the clear blue sky. The leaves still clung to the trees, and those scattered along the ground were as vibrantly hued as ever. Rich reds, golden ambers, and warm orange tones carpeted the world—an extravagance tossed away by nature every year. Such is the bounty of the forest. Vera inhaled the scents of the scene around her. Crisp air mingled with the warm, faintly sweet humus of the earth, and she sighed contentedly.

"I'm never sure what my favorite season is, but autumn is hard to beat. In the city, I hardly noticed the changes. Here, there's something different every day."

"You don't miss your old life?" Orville asked.

"Hardly," she said firmly. "Oh, sure, there were perks. But on the whole, I can't imagine going back to that. Funny that Bradley Marvel thought the mere mention of the city would get my interest . . ."

"Wait, what?"

Whoops. So far Vera had deliberately avoided telling Orville the details of the wolf's clumsy maneuverings, mostly to avoid bloodshed. But now, with Marvel safely out of the area—

and hopefully back in the city—she could tell all. So she gave
Orville a shortened but truthful account of events. His expression grew fiercer with every revelation.

"He wanted you to leave Shady Hollow and work as a . . .
flunky? For *him*?"

"Oh, and to date him as well." Vera shrugged. "It was not a
compelling offer, and I told him so. Then I told him to get out
of town."

"Wise." Orville's voice took on the growl it got when he felt
strongly about anything. "And better tell Lenore that he should
wait a good long while before coming through on another
book tour."

Vera laughed. "I will. Despite the sales, I think Lenore would
prefer not to see him in the shop ever again."

They walked through the quiet town, through a patch of
woodland, and then on to the neighborhood nestled on the
shore of Mirror Lake. The sky clouded over as they walked,
drawing the color out of the world.

Without speaking a word about it, they took the path to
that grand house where Dorothy Springfield now lived alone.
It was too early for a social call, so they simply continued
toward the lakeshore.

It was very quiet that morning, since most creatures had
chosen to nestle into the warmth of their homes, enjoying a
leisurely breakfast or sipping hot cocoa by the fire. Vera noticed
only a few well-bundled residents hurrying to and fro.

Over the silver, silken surface of Mirror Lake floated little
white flakes that began to kiss the quiet water. Vera gazed up
into the new mass of clouds above, which had sailed in without her even realizing it. She murmured, "Lenore said snow is
on the way."

"She'd know," said Orville. "Trust a bird to give you the weather right."

"That's not all she's good at predicting," Vera replied, smiling at him. "She knew you'd win the election!"

The giant bear actually looked bashful. "Might be better to say Meade lost it. Folks wanted a change."

"They wanted a chief," she countered. "You're the one they turn to when they get scared. You brought a murderer to justice. A very slippery murderer, at that."

Now Orville gave a snort. "Didn't do all that on my own. Folks know that Miss Vera Vixen will solve any case she gets her cute little nose into."

Vera sighed happily, thinking they did make a good team.

After a moment, Orville said, "Suppose I got to get to work sometime today. Let's walk back to Shady Hollow proper. Before I go to the station, we can stop at Joe's for a cup of coffee and a slice of pie. I'm buying."

"Oh, no," Vera said. "As a reporter, I can't let the law pay for my treats. What will folks think of me then?"

"All right, you buy my pie and coffee, and I'll buy yours. And if anyone asks, we'll say we did the opposite."

"Collusion?"

"Compromise."

She smiled. "It's a deal."

The End

Acknowledgments

Between us, we have constructed a world of woodland creatures who live, work, and murder in a delightful small community. But the creation of the Shady Hollow Mystery series was most definitely a group effort.

At the outset, Nicholas Tulach served as our first publisher at Hammer & Birch, going above and beyond to get our stories into book form and out into the world.

We are eternally grateful to our former boss and current friend Daniel Goldin, owner and proprietor of Boswell Book Company in Milwaukee. He was one of our first readers and a tireless cheerleader for the books, hand selling them to anyone who crossed his path and stood still long enough. May all authors be so lucky.

We would also like to thank our friends and family who bought the books, attended our events, and were kind enough to tell us how much they enjoyed the stories. This love and encouragement kept us writing and helped us explore the world of Shady Hollow, allowing us to discover new characters and places in every book.

Many thanks go to Jason Gobble, publishing rep extraordinaire, for being awesome. We can never thank you enough for your generous support of these books in particular and for being a champion of books in general.

And we must thank Caitlin Landuyt, editor at Vintage Books & Anchor Books, who gave these mysteries a fresh launch into the world and fulfilled dreams we didn't even know we had.

Additionally, Sharon would like to say: Thank you to my beloved husband, Mark, who believes in me and supports me in everything I do.

And Jocelyn says: A huge thanks to my parents, who raised me on PBS murder mysteries, taught me to love reading, and didn't flinch when I chose to major in English. These books are for you.

And thank you, Nick, for always being there. You are without doubt the best thing to happen to me, and I love you more than cheese.

Read more from
Juneau Black

The Shady Hollow Mystery Series

"A cross between *Twin Peaks*
and *Fantastic Mr. Fox.*"
—Milwaukee Record